CARNY KILL

CARNY KILL

by Robert Edmond Alter

WILDSIDE PRESS

To
PAT STADLEY

Carny Kill

Published by Wildside Press LLC
wildsidepress.com | bcmystery.com

Chapter One

It was one of those tourist traps that have turned the coast of Florida into a glittering facade. They hide the naked sight of the hundreds of thousands of voracious cash registers behind the tinsel. That way the innocent tourists won't be stampeded into running for cover in fear for their wallets.

This place was on the outskirts, on the tidelands, where acreage is cheap. It was a big, bristling, brawling take-off on the Disneyland idea out in Southern Cal. You might almost call it a steal.

It was owned and operated by an old carny man named Robert Cochrane, and he was a pretty canny Irishman. If Disney had a Jungle Ride, Cochrane had a Swamp Ride. The Swiss Family Robinson Tree House at Disneyland became the Tarzan House at Neverland. That was the name of the trap. Neverland. Remember Peter Pan's fun-and-games island?

Like most of those places that are designed for the tourist who wanders around with money falling out of his pockets, it looked fine on top, impressive. Then you start scratching the surface and the dirt you find under your fingernails is the same grime you'll find in any clipjoint.

That's why I felt at home.

They had a regular old fashioned carnival attraction tucked behind a monstrosity called Dracula's Castle—where all kinds of wired spooks sprang at you with ear-splitting screams and where your girl's skirt was blown up around her ears so all the sailors and pimply-faced high-school dropouts could gawk at her panties. I made for it like a homing pigeon.

But something was wrong. It was like I'd walked into a familiar room and found that somebody had moved a couple pieces of furniture out of place.

They had the illusion show and the shooting gallery and the fat lady and the tattooed man and the stripshow.

Everything was there but it was out of tune. The stripshow barker for example. He was as noisy and as flashy as he should be but he wasn't trying to turn his tip with that air of insistent urgency you usually expect to find in a sideshow. He seemed to be making a joke of it.

Then I got it. It was all a joke, a part of the facade. The carny attraction was only there for atmosphere. So Ma could turn to Pa and say, "Why it's just like a regular sideshow, ain't it, Elmo?" Just good wholesome fun. Something else Cochrane had learned from Mr.Disney.

A soldier and two girls and a man and wife with their two girls, and then two girls who didn't seem to belong to anybody, were all ganged around the shooting gallery and the soldier was making an embarrassed sap of himself by missing all the little white rabbits as they glided by on their pivots.

One of the soldier's girls turned and looked at me—that sort of under-and-around look that's been handed down from girl to girl for God knows how many thousands of years—and she had on a sweater that must have belonged to her little sister, it was that tight, and she might have been all of sixteen.

I decided to make the soldier look even better.

"Step aside, folks," I said in my barker voice. "Let the man see the rabbit."

The op behind the counter had the kind of mute, predatory face that belonged in a shooting gallery. He gave me a quick flat look and handed me a twentytwo in exchange for my quarter.

The soldier didn't think much of me. He said so with his eyes. I grinned at him. Then I winked at the girl on his left. The one with the sweater that wouldn't stop.

I looked at the twentytwo and it looked all right. Then I bapped at the first little rabbit and turned him aboutface on his pivot. It seemed to be an honest rifle. When the rabbit slid out of his burrow again I went to work on him and kept him turning right-left, right-left until the magazine was empty.

I handed the rifle back to the op.

"Where do I find The Man?" I asked.

His eyes drifted to the left as though he were thinking

about something else—anything, including reaching for the billy he probably kept under the counter.

"Something wrong?" he asked quietly.

"No beef," I told him. "Need a job."

"Carny?"

"Yeah." I named a couple of outfits.

"Spiel?"

"Um. And sleight of hand. The usual."

His eyes flicked at me again. Then he raised himself against the counter and called over our heads to a girl who was passing through the outer crowd.

"Billie! 'Mere, huh?"

This girl wasn't sixteen. She wasn't wearing a sweater. She looked as sharp as a New York City model. She had floss candy hair that made you hungry. She stopped and looked toward us inquiringly, then walked our way, her highheels clicking rhythmically on the cement.

That's when the soldier decided to show his girls just who was as tough as a horseshoe around there.

"You wink at her, buddy?" He meant the sweater girl.

"No," I said.

He came a little closer and managed to give the movement a touch of swagger.

"Yeah but I seen you," he said.

"Then why ask me about it—if you sawed me?"

"Listen, buddy," he said.

I didn't want to fight him. There was no point in it. I was pretty sure I could take him, the way a fighter can sometimes tell with his opponent the first moment he comes in against him. There's no profit in proving something to yourself that you already know.

I said,"Let's forget about it," and I turned to face the girl with the cottoncandy hair.

She was looking at my face and her eyes slid over my right shoulder and widened a little. I guess the soldier had decided to exhibit some muscle about then, because I heard the shooting gallery op say, "Ixnay, soldier. Or I'll have three guards on you before you can say Jesus."

The soldier said something about my mother's marital status and gathered up his girls and left. I wasn't paying any attention. I was looking at the girl called Billie.

You meet a girl like this, who looked as if she had just stepped out of the center-spread of *Playboy* magazine with her clothes on, and you can damn near feel your lousy fiftytwo-dollar suit grow wrinkles and you wish to God you had shaved later in the day instead of the first thing in the morning.

"He wants to see Rob. A job. Take him, huh?" The shooting gallery op finished his telegram message and this Billie looked at me again and said, "Sure."

I said thanks to the shooting gallery op and Billie and I walked off together.

One of the things I liked about her is that she *didn't* use that wouldn't-you-like-to-lay-me look that's been handed down for thousands of years. When she looked at me it was straight on. It wasn't cold or to hell with you, buster. It was impersonal and it was honest.

"Billie," I said. "That's a perfect name for a prostitute."

"What's that crack supposed to mean?" A little fire came into her eyes. They were gold-flecked. It was still daylight. That's how I could tell the color of her eyes.

"No inference meant," I said. "That's just the way your name struck me. If I were going to write a book and I wanted a whore in it, I'd call her Billie."

She smiled. "Too stereotyped. Too obvious. I'd fool everyone and call her an old-fashioned name. Like Emily."

I didn't tell her I'd once known a whore named Emily. She hadn't been old-fashioned though.

The barker on the illusion show bally platform was an adenoidal-looking man who used his adenoma-voice as part of his stock in trade. He was spieling to a group of marks about the spider lady.

"She scrabbles, she climbs, she spins a web."

Then I looked at him again. He was looking over his marks at me. I didn't say anything or make a sign. I kept on walking with Billie. But she had noticed.

"Something?" she asked incuriously.

"Uh-uh." There was no sense in telling her that Bill Duff and I once worked in a carny together. That Bill Duff used to hang around my wife like a bee around honey. That Bill Duff lost an eyetooth one night when I lost my patience.

"What do you do around here, Billie?" I asked.

"I'm one of the nautch girls. I do a specialty dance. Only it's more the Twist than anything Far East."

"I'll bet you're good."

She smiled up at me. I'm fairly tall. So was she but even in her spike heels I was up to her.

"I'll bet you bet," she said.

"I'll come see you in action sometime," I said.

"Not if Rob gives you a job you won't." She was firm about that.

They had a tavern which really wasn't a tavern and they called it the Klondike. It was right out of the 1898 gold rush. Lots of Yukon atmosphere. They had a floorshow where the girls in the big feathered hats whirled around and threw up their skirts and saluted the audience with their bottoms. A sort of halfassed cancan. They served only soft drinks. It was pretty cute.

Billie took me around to the back. There was a closed door with the usual mysterious word *Private* on it, and she said: "You'll find Rob upstairs."

"All right," I said. "Now I know where to find Rob. Where do I find you?"

"I told you where I work."

"You said I was too young to see such sights."

She smiled and it was a very pretty thing and I wanted to reach out and take hold of her and start making love to her right there in front of the private door behind the Klondike.

"I'll know where to find you," she said. "If you get the job. The word gets around." Then she said, "Oh. You didn't mention your name."

"I never do if I can help it. So I go by the first half of my last. Thax."

"Thaxton?"

"Uh-huh."

"I'm Billie Peeler."

I looked at her. It was too much of a coincidence to be true. She laughed.

"My agent gave it to me. Only took him an hour of brain-racking to come up with it."

"I figured."

"Well," she said, "I hope you get the job."
"Well," I said, "it doesn't really matter, does it?"
Her greengold eyes gave me a look of mild speculation.
"That's entirely up to you—Thax."
I wasn't sure I got that. Then I looked at her eyes again and I was sure. And it did matter whether I got that job or not.

Chapter Two

This Robert Cochrane reminded me of a character out of *The Informer.* As Irish as Paddy's potato. Built like one, too. Big, round, rough. He didn't have the faith-and-bejasus brogue though, which was a shame. Then he would have been complete. He must have been getting on to sixty.

"C'mon in and grab a seat. That one—where I can look at you. Carny man, huh?" He grinned at me like a Halloween pumpkin.

"The word really does get around," I said, and sat in a chair on the other side of his desk. "Or does it show on my face?"

"Gabby gave me a buzz," he explained. "I like to keep in touch."

"Gabby" I said. "Oh, the shooting gallery op." It was one of those ironic reversals. The guy who hardly ever opens his mouth is usually tagged Gabby.

"Spielers I don't need," Cochrane told me right off. "They're a dime a dozen."

"So are strippers," I said. "But who ever turns a pro down?"

The light went on in his pumpkin face again.

"You're good, huh? What have you done?"

I named a few outfits I had worked for. Then I said, "My wife used to have an act. I spieled for her."

He was studying me now.

"What's your name?"

"L. M. Thaxton. Thax is good enough."

His grin came back. "I'll bet that first initial covers up a doozy."

I smiled. "How would you like to be called Leslie?"

"What about this sleight of hand?" he wondered. "You good at it?"

I hunched forward and put both my elbows on the desk, picked up a number four pyramid-shaped sinker he used as a paperweight in my left hand and held it up to him. Then I made a flicker of motion with my right forefinger and the split instant his eyes trembled I ducked my left hand at the wrist and showed him my open palm and he was staring at an empty hand.

A real legerdemain artist is born, not made. Constant practice is vital, sure. But it doesn't add up to a good goddam if the sense of prestidigitation isn't inherent in the performer. The big trick is in directing the attention of your audience at the instant you substitute one thing for another. I had directed Cochrane's attention to my right hand when I shot the sinker down my left sleeve.

Cochrane was beaming like a kid. Funny thing about him—as old as he was and as long as he'd been around illusionists, he still got a kick out of that sort of thing.

"It's up your left sleeve, huh?" he said.

"Sure—it was," I said and I shot my left arm straight out at him and turned over my fist and opened it and it was still empty. He smiled and looked in my right hand and took back his paperweight.

"You've got the knack," he admitted, "but . . ." He thought about it for a bit. Then— "Here's a thought. You good at the shell game?"

I said I was and he said all right, he would put me in the carnival attraction with a stand and the shell game, to add to the atmosphere. Then he became serious.

"This ain't the old carny you and I knew," he warned me. "We don't pick the marks up by the heels and shake 'em till they're dry anymore. Times have changed."

"Yes they have," I said. "The shooting gallery op still keeps a sap under the counter and you still pay the law blind money to ignore the nautch girls."

He grinned. "You're guessing. Sure, we've got a lot of old time carnys working this lot, and they're as sharp as ever. But once you get around you'll notice we got high-school and college kids working here. Nice clean kids that keep the atmosphere homey."

He looked at me as if he were trying to see inside me, see what made me spin.

"I want it to stay that way, Thax." He meant it.

For a moment I felt an old familiar unease, and I wondered if he had heard about me. Then I figured probably not—otherwise he would want to kick it around before he hired me. There were some outfits up north that wouldn't touch me with an elephant gaff.

"Sure," I said. "I won't give you any grief."

I meant it. I liked him.

Then he named a price and I didn't think much of it and I gave one with a better name, which he countered, and I countered it, and we settled somewhere in between, and then he gave me a card that said I was employed by the Cochrane Enterprises.

"How's the grouch bag holding?" he asked.

"All right. I've got a few bucks."

Damn few. Five bucks was the truth. But I didn't want to start out by touching the boss.

"Got a place to sack?" he asked. "There's a bunkhouse around behind the Watusi Village. Some of the boys use it."

I knew those bunkhouses. They're used by the rummies who swamp up the lot and by the alky-paralyzed geek. Though this place wouldn't have one because there is nothing homey about a geek's atmosphere.

"I'll make out," I told him.

"All right, Thax. I'll have Gabby set you up a stand. Keep your nose clean."

"Like a whistle," I said. I really did like him.

It was dusk when I came out and Neverland was full of clamor. Cochrane's lot got a good play.

The place was laid out like a wagonwheel with a big garden in the hub. It had a fountain with colored lights and liquid music coming out of the water and that sort of thing.

The Coke and popcorn and ice-cream vendors wheeled their barrows up and down the flowered lanes and hawked their appeals to the common hunger and thirst of the citizenry. Little, overpainted, short-skirted highschool girls ran around in shrieking batches with armloads of kewpie dolls and peanuts and floss candy, and small gangs of pimply, shaggy-haired teenage boys prowled doggedly after them, laughing and smirking and desperately trying to show everyone just how goddam rough and manly they really were by yelling *Aw hell* and *My ass* in their puberty-shrill voices.

And the luck boys were there too. It's easy to spot them when you know what to look for. There was one—a big curly-haired, rose-cheeked man who might have passed for a prosperous lawyer—who was holding up his hand to attract the attention of a more or less middle-aged group of marks.

"The management has requested me to warn you that there's been a report of a pickpocket in here this evening. Please, ladies and gentlemen, watch out for your wallets and purses. And *please* do not hesitate to inform one of the uniformed guards if you should happen to notice this man. The management will pay a reward for his apprehension. Thank you."

It was an old dodge. I grinned at the luckboy and held up my five dollar bill and put it back in my pocket.

I went over and joined the gang of lusty-eyed marks in front of the kootch bally stand, telling myself I might as well get some use out of my Neverland card. But the truth was I wanted to see that dance of Billie's. The girl who collected tickets gave me a funny little look when I flashed my card but I didn't think anything about it.

The little theater was dark, except for the lighted stage, and it looked like some fairy designer's idea of a lush seraglio with all the Far East draperies on the walls and the scimitars and the swords with the rippled blades and the high domed ceiling with luminous stars painted on it.

The orchestra sat gook-legged on a Persian rug and they were dressed to look like Malay pirates I guess. They had two-three wood drums and a couple of pick and twang gut-strung boxes that looked like the barbaric cousins of the guitar. And there was a horn.

Three nautch girls in skimpy harem-type outfits were on stage and they went through their gyrations like they weren't being paid enough for it, showing a lot of meaty white thigh and breast. It wasn't much. I found myself a vacant seat in the back where I figured Billie wouldn't be able to see me in the dark.

Then she came out and they hit her with a pink spot. She was wearing some lawbreaking sheer turquoise veils and a lot of bangles and heavy makeup and that was about it. She was incalculably voluptuous.

One of the drums said *domm* and she slapped her hands and hip-slung a hole in culture that would take a decade of hardbound morality to shore up.

It had a lot of the Yankee Go Go in it and maybe some of the South American Mandango and damn little that was indigenous to the Far East. But that was all right because the marks hadn't paid the price of admission to see a National Geographic type show. They simply wanted to see near naked girls gyrate.

It began with a surge that vacuumed us out of the darkened room, out of the night and Neverland, and were spellbound and tense as we went drifting along on a throbbing plain of savage fantasia.

Her floss hair flying, her hips whirling on an oiled spine, shoulders arched and arms out and hands fondling invisible and suggestive objects, she started to shed her veils, tossing them off with an air of ecstatic abandonment. The last one hung poised on her tremulous breasts, and she reached for it and tore it down to her waist and it clung there for a moment, tight to her damp form as she whirled and whirled, and then it flew off.

The drumbeat pulsated fever in our blood and rushed us through a wild panorama of paganism. It was unabashed desire swept by flesh and pink light and throbbing sound. It shattered in the physical and regrouped with a turquoise and gold spurt. It fired the senses and split the soul. It ended with a rush and threw us brutally back to the world and the night and the little darkened room. It left us shaky and sweaty and maybe even a little afraid. Afraid of ourselves, I suppose. Or of our desire. Or that our desire would go unassuaged.

There was a lot of applause for Billie, except from the female portion of the audience who looked rather arch and cold about the whole thing. Billie was good. I don't mean she would ever end up as Fred Astaire's partner, but for a bareface sex dance she had it.

The girlfriends of the male marks were too disdainful and above it all to comment on the dance, but some of the wives had a thing or two to say and they didn't mind who heard them. The husbands seemed rather reticent and averted their eyes as they filed out of the room. One heavy woman with jowls like a fat bulldog's stormed by me dragging her mousy spouse in her overly perfumed wake.

"Shameless!" she hissed at him in a stevedore's voice. "The most shameless exhibition I've ever witnessed. I can't imagine why you insisted on seeing such a vulgar display, Walter."

Poor little Walter sent me a prideless glance of despair and murmured, "Yes, honey."

I didn't get off free either. The strip barker tagged me as I was walking out.

"Thaxton? Billie Peeler wants to see you a minute."

"Me? Why?"

"I wouldn't know, Jack. But be sure and look me up and tell me all about it when you find out. Promise?"

Then he grinned at me in a nice way so I didn't go ahead and call him a smart bastard as I'd started to.

Billie came through a side door wearing a wrapper that covered her up like a nun, and I could see from her eyes that she was about to be peeved. The barker gave me a wink and patted Billie where he shouldn't and went off about his own business.

"Did Rob Cochrane give you a job?"

It was no good my saying no because the ticket girl must have already told her I had a Neverland card.

"Sure and he did that, the darlin' bhoy."

"Then why did you have to come sticking your banjo eyes in here?" Now she was mad.

"Why not?" I already knew but I wanted her to tell me.

"You know damn well why. It's all right for a bunch of marks to goggle at me when I look like Eve, but it's something else if someone I know pays to do it."

"I'm safe then. I didn't pay. I used my Peter Pan card"

"Thax—"

I grinned at her. "I'm just kidding, Billie. I'm sorry. Really."

"Well—" her voice wasn't as peevish now, "you should have known better. That little bitch Sandy who collects the tickets saw us talking earlier on the lot. She thought it was very funny that you should sneak in to see me in the altogether as soon as you got a free pass."

"I'll send her a bomb for Easter," I promised.

She looked at me and we smiled at each other and then for a long moment we didn't seem to know what to say next.

"Well," she said, finally, "I've got to get ready for the next show." She started to turn away but stopped, and she said, "I'm really glad you got the job, Thax."

So was I. At least right then I was glad.

I decided to grab a bite before I scouted up a flop for the night, and I went up a path to a quaint little restaurant called the Queen Anne Cottage.

I was jostled on the steps by some people coming out and I told one of them—the biggest man in the group—to watch it, buster. He asked me how I'd like a bent nose to watch and I asked him wouldn't he rather wait until he had more than three friends to help him and he said he wasn't going to need any goddam help and then his wife or his secretary or whatever she was broke it up.

When I put my hand in my pocket my five was gone. Those luck boys were damn thorough.

I was standing on the porch muttering filthy words to myself when a highschool or college kid wearing a red-and-white guide uniform stepped up to me and asked was I Mr. Thaxton, sir?

"So what?" I wanted to know.

"Mrs. Cochrane wants to see you, sir." He was really a very polite boy. One of Cochrane's nice clean kids.

"Mrs. Cochrane?" I didn't get it.

"The owner's wife, sir." He was very patient with me. Too patient.

"Look, son," I said. "I can add two and two. But why's she want to see me?"

"I'm sure I don't know, sir. She simply asked me to—"

"Yeah, yeah. So where do I find the owner's wife?"

"She has a suite of rooms above this restaurant, sir."

Everybody who was anybody seemed to live and work

over some kind of joint in this place. The nice clean boy told me to go around to the back, where I would find a door marked *Private*. Naturally.

I thanked him, and then I added, "Oh—and don't call me Sir. I work here just like you."

"Yes sir," he said promptly. "I know that."

Very polite. But that sir business made me feel my thirty-two years. Maybe more.

I went around back and opened the door that always had to say *Private* when it was around back and went up a maroon carpeted stairway that was walled in with way-out paintings that made you feel like you were trying to climb out of the paint pots of a surrealist artist's night mare.

I came to another door. It didn't say Private so I opened it and stepped into a blaze of light. It was like stepping into an interrogation room. Some kind of baby spot stood back in a corner and hit me all over with a brilliant pink light.

I had a quick, vague impression of Swedish modern as I put up an arm to ward off that damn glare, and then something went *ssst* right by my head and *thh-ok* in the paneled wall.

I was already on my way to the floor.

It was reasonably soft—about two inches of thick carpeting and as woolly as a fat lamb. All I hurt was my left elbow. Then I turned a little and glanced up at the knife jutting out from the wall. It was no longer than a butcher knife and it had a mother-of-pearl handle and no hilt-guard.

I knew that kind of knife. In fact there was a time when I used to have bad dreams about them. My wife used to throw them back when we were in carny together.

A laugh that was a sort of throaty tinkle, if there is such a laugh, came out of the darkness beyond the baby spot. And I knew who I was going to see when the rest of the lights went on.

They went on and I saw I was right about the Swedish modern motif and about the possessor of the unusual laugh. My ex-wife was reclined on some kind of cushy sofa that seemed to be made entirely of satin pillows. She was wearing one of those gold-glittery outfits with the toreador jacket and skintight pants. And gold sandals. And her toenails too. Gold.

She had changed her hair. It used to make Monroe's platinum head look like dishwater blonde. Now she was flame headed. But her face hadn't changed in five years. The same cold, sensual, calculating look that I had fallen in love with when I was twenty and stupid was still there.

I looked to be sure she didn't have another knife handy before I picked myself off the rug.

"You'd never draw a crowd with that toss, May," I said. "It was off a foot."

"You lying sonofabitch, darling." She smiled at me. "It took the peachfuzz off your ear. Do you want to change your pants?"

"No," I said. "I'm still wearing my diapers."

I pulled the knife loose. It gave me a bit of a struggle. May always did have a beautiful throwing arm. That's what used to worry me—when we'd have our fights.

The knife had perfect balance. No matter how you tossed it the harpoon-sharp blade always led the way to the target. The mother-of-pearl handles had been her trademark. She had always been a great one for classy show. And it looked like she had made it. Mrs. Robert Cochrane. She couldn't be but twenty-five years younger than the canny Irishman.

I wagged the blade at her. "Fun and games, huh May?"

"You know goddam well I could have put your eye out if I'd wanted to, sweetie," she said sweetly. "I've kept my hand in."

I was a believer. May always kept her hand in, and not just with her knives.

"Way in," I said and nodded around at the big, cushy room. "Some opulence."

"Never mind your goddam book words, Thax," she said. She never could stand big words. At least not when I used them.

"A nice mark," I amended. "Very nice."

It was the freaky coincidence of the thing—my ending up at Neverland and her being Mrs. Never Never—that surprised me. Not the fact that she had made out like a foreign loan. Some people, especially some females, are slated for affluence no matter how far down the social strata they start. The crystal gazers like to call it Kismet.

May had come out of one of those naughty houses they

used to have in San Berdoo, California. I think the district was called D Street. But it hadn't phased her. The first time she was old enough to recognize the significance of the two-dollar bill one of the truck driver customers handed her mother she knew exactly what it was that made the world go around and she climbed aboard to get her share of the spin.

I had been a husky young carny kid with a good spiel and she had used me for just as long as I was worth anything to her. When she outgrew me she started looking around for a way to dump me. And I had found her the way.

But what really amazed me was that Irishman—Robert Cochrane, her husband. He must have known who I was once I told him my name, and he must have known about the jam I got into when May and I were working together for the Brody outfit. Yet he hadn't said a word. He had gone ahead and hired me. Funny guy. Unless May had held out on him.

"You tell Cochrane about you and me?" I asked her.

"Sure," she said. "When I first came to him. *I* have nothing to hide. Anyhow, he knew my name. Word gets around, you know."

"Jesus if it doesn't. Everybody seems to know about me like I'd been here all my life. You have anything to do with hiring me?"

May smiled at me. Call it that, anyhow.

"I didn't even know you were on the lot, darling, till Bill Duff told me."

"Good old Bill," I said. "Did he go to that dentist I recommended before I clipped his eyetooth?"

May kept right on smiling at me. She didn't say anything.

"Cozy for you and Bill, huh?" I suggested. "This setup."

"Duff showed up just like you did," she said in a stainless-steel voice. "Broke and whimpering for a job. Rob gave him the job because Rob can't turn down a carny buddy with an empty grouch bag. I would have told Duff to go take a flying leap at the spider lady."

"From what I understand he already had way before we met him," I said. But I said it out of habit—automatic reaction. I was still entranced by the knowledge that the Irishman had hired me even though he knew all about me. A very funny guy.

"Well," I said, "it doesn't really matter."

"So you always say, sweetie," May said.

I came back to the Swedish modern suite above the Queen Anne Cottage.

"Look, May. Times have been soso with me." I fluctuated one hand palm-down in mid air to illustrate the soso-ness of my times. "I need the job. Are you going to queer it?"

She started to uncoil like a cat on the sofa. She reached a very pale gold-tipped hand up to me.

"Rob does all the hiring and firing, sweetie. I wouldn't dream of saying a word. Come here."

"Why?"

"Kiss me."

"Why?"

"Curiosity."

She had something there. I was curious too, to see if it would be the same. Five years is a long time. I sank into the satin pillows and she put a hand on my neck and I put one on her waist and we pulled in. Then she opened her mouth and I covered it with mine and her tongue started to leap, and by damn if it *wasn't* the same. The same as when I was a husky young carny kid of twenty. Not the same as those last few years before she threw me over.

My left hand immediately grew bored because what kick can a hand get-out of holding a woman's waist? So I let it do what it wanted to do and it went sliding upward to find something of a more tactile interest. Once it found it May pulled back.

"I said kiss, sweetie," she reminded me.

"You didn't say kiss what though, did you?" I grinned at her.

She straightened up and went pat-pat at her too perfect fiery hair.

"I rather imagine, darling, that you are going to get yourself into sex trouble again. You're certainly showing all the indications."

"Well, it doesn't matter, does it?" I said. I got up and put my tie in order. "Troublewise, they ain't getting no virgin."

"You can say that again," May said. "Run along now, sweetie, and see if you can keep your pants zipped for a whole week."

She had meant it when she said it was curiosity. There really hadn't been any great passion behind her wet kiss. It was habit with her. You don't melt an iceberg with a blowtorch because there just isn't that much juice in a blowtorch.

"See you, May." I started for the door.

"Yes."

That's all she said. Just yes.

Chapter Three

The big luckboy with the lawyerlike aspect was hovering near the front of the Queen Anne Cottage, like a shark finning around a ship to pick up its garbage. He was looking for another likely group of marks.

I went over and buttonholed him. He was my big and looked handy, so I didn't mind pasting him if I had to.

"You and I need a talk back in the alley," I said.

He started to grin and to reach into his pocket at the same time.

"Hell man," he said, "I didn't know you belonged. Should have guessed though, the way you were in on the know."

He fished out my five and passed it over without hard feelings.

"You were asking for it though, you know," he said.

"That's right, I was," I admitted. "Was it the big guy that I bollixed with on the steps?"

"Hell no. That was just another mark. But Eddy was in the group and got him at the same time." The luckboy chuckled. "I couldn't myself. I had to put Eddy on you, once you'd challenged me."

"That Eddy must be good," I said as I handed the luckboy back his wallet.

He looked at the slab of leather like he had never seen it before. When he put it in his pocket I gave him back his watch.

"*Kayriced,*" he whispered. "A pro of the first water. Look, Thaxton, you're in the wrong racket. You don't want to play house with walnut shells with a natural talent like that! Rob Cochrane practically gives us oldtimers a free hand. Within reason, that is."

"My name, racket and everything," I said. "You know it all already."

"Yeah," he said absently. "Word gets around. But look—"

"Uh-uh," I said. "It ain't in my line. But thanks for the offer."

I went into the Queen Anne and had a steak and showed my card to the cashier and she knocked the bill down to half. She was another one of those nice clean student employees who helped gloss over the fleecing with homey atmosphere, and she looked at me in a way that suggested she was starting to practice the look that had been handed down for thousands of years. But I ignored it, more or less, because I had promised Cochrane.

Anyhow, I had Billie on my mind.

I don't care how you cut it or how sexually degenerate you are, there's no man who can hold more than one thought in his mind at a given moment. That goes for thinking about girls. Sure you can love or want or need two or three all at once, but you can only actually activate the imagery of one at a time.

Try it. Picture yourself buried under a mound of naked girls. Strive as you will you can only imagine what *one* girl is doing at a time no matter how instantaneous your erotic thoughts fly.

That's how Billie struck me. All the rest of them in this great sensual world were suddenly secondary. It could be that in time, a hell of a lot of time, I would get around to a small percentage of them, but right now, Billie was the sum of the equation. Or something like that.

I wandered about for a couple of hours just to get the lay of the lot, but I got tired of it in a little while. Like most carney folk I don't like people as people but only as marks. Somebody you can trim for a dime or a buck or a bundle. If you break them down and feed them to me one by one, then maybe there will be a few I will like as individuals. But not when they flow past you like bawling cattle. Who needs a stampede?

Along about eleven thirty some hairy-lunged college boy climbed up to the lookout tower in the Viking Camp and blew through a horn that was ten feet long and suspended by rawhide thongs.

Hooo! the horn said in a fat dismal voice. *Hooo!*

That meant the marks should start to clear out. Which suited me. I had to find a spot to grab some shuteye.

In my wandering I had seriously eyed Tarzan's tree house. It was summer and the breeze blowing off the sea was mild and this movie-copied replica of Tarzan's home was free. I had even showed my Open-sesame card and gone up in the bamboo-ribbed elevator to look the tree house over.

I had noted a zebra-skin bed with elephant tusks for posts, where Me Tarzan and You Jane had supposedly enjoyed their connubial bliss, and I had had to chuckle when I recalled that sex-frustrated oldmaid librarian in California who had raised such a stink about the Tarzan books simply because she hadn't bothered to read enough of them to learn that Tarzan and Jane had been legally married in the second book.

Anyhow, the connubial jungle bed looked good enough to me. You Jane or no You Jane. So I hung around there until the crowd petered out.

This Tarzan house overlooked the Swamp Ride and they had about nine nice clean kids who ran the boats through the circular swamp. One of them came by me with a polite smile and a face full of freckles.

"All closed up for the night, sir," he said.

I told him my name was Thax and showed him my wonderful Never Never card and that made him more polite than ever.

"I haven't seen you around here, sir. Are you new?"

Well, what are you going to do? If they *have* to call you sir how can you stop them? Beat 'em on the head with a stick? I smiled at him like foxy grandpa and admitted I was new.

"Well gosh," he said and he actually looked distressed. "I'd show you the Swamp Ride, except that—"

"Except that you have a tasty girl waiting." He probably had his little old grayhaired mother waiting but I wanted to make him feel good.

"Don't worry about it," I said. "It doesn't really matter."

I shooed him off, and when the coast was clear I went up

the plank steps that curved around a phony tree like a scutellated snake, and I wobbled over the swaying bamboo footbridge to Tarzan's house.

It was really quite something when you thought about it—the fact that all the leaves on the two trees were fake and that each one had been placed on by hand. But I didn't think too much about it right then. I was deadbeat and that steak in my stomach still needed some repose time to digest in.

It was dark in Tarzan's house, but there were still some arc lights on down in Neverland and the bamboo and thatch walls let in light the way a sieve lets in water. I could see my way to bed.

There was another smaller bed against the other wall. That was Cheeta's bed. The bright little highschool girl in the skimpy leopard skin who was in charge of the tree house had told us so earlier. All the Ma's and Pa's had thought it was a great one. The Pa's had chuckled and the Ma's had said *Oooh* in that endearing way they have.

I didn't mind sleeping with a monkey, as long as he stayed on his side of the room. I was whipped. I even thought I dreamed that Cheeta swung in through his window and dropped into his bed in the late dark night.

It didn't matter. At least I didn't think it did.

I don't know how long that godawful noise had been going on before it woke me up, but when I finally consciously heard it all I could think of was a thunderstorm.

That's what a gator sounds like when he bellows. When he plants all four stumpy legs in the mud and really let go his voice has a sort of *barrr-ooom* to it like distant thunder.

It was morning. I looked at my wristwatch. Eight. Then I sat up. What else can you do when someone stars yelling for help?

"Help! Somebody! C'mere!"

The voice was thin and urgent and some distance off. I went out on the porch and looked down at the Swamp Ride. It was laid out in a huge figure eight but I couldn't see all of the water-ways because the jungly growth was too dense. I could see one of the little powered swamp boats scooting back to the dock though, and all the yelling seemed to be coming from it.

I went back inside and got my pants.

A couple of the rummy sweep-up men were wobbling toward me when I reached the Swamp Ride gate, and two or three of the guide girls were coming on the run too. I went around the closed ticket booth and stepped out on the dock.

The powerboat was just pulling in and my friend Freckles was at the wheel. His freckles looked like measles against the ashen color of his face. He was scared wetless.

"Oh my God!" he gasped when he saw me. "It's awful! Just awful! He's dead!"

I jumped into the boat with him, nearly scalping myself on the roof rod. They had eight or nine of those little boats and each one of them was built like the *African Queen*—with the canvas tarp for a roof.

I got Freckles by the shoulders before he could come apart at the seams. He was pretty hysterical but I didn't slap him like they always do in the movies and on TV because it never works in real life. It just seems to jar loose more hysteria in the nut.

"Somebody's got to do something!" Freckles yelled in my face, spit and all. "My God those gators!"

"Yeah yeah," I yelled back at him. "But who? Who's dead? Where is he?"

"Yes! Yes!" the kid said frantically insistent. *"He's dead!* I'm telling you *he's dead!* He's in the water and those gators—"

I wasn't getting anywhere, and if I'd had any sense I would have gotten out of there because it wasn't any of my business. But who has any sense these days?

"Okay. Okay. Show me." I gave him a shake. "Show me where."

I could feel him shrinking in my hands.

"I never saw a dead man before." His voice was hoarse now, gaspy. "It's terrible!"

"Yeah. All right, kid. Get out." I didn't need a hysteric on my hands. "Where is it?"

Freckles pointed across the bow at a jungle-arched waterway. Then he scrambled up on the dock. More and more people were gathering with question marks for faces.

There was nothing to those little boats. Freckles had left

the power on and I gave it a healthy goose and spun the wheel and went ripping down the waterway at about half a knot an hour. The governor on that boat must have been as tight as a virgin's something or other.

There was very little about the Swamp Ride that was phony. All the palmettos and sweet gums and tupelos and the intricate network of prehensile vines were real. There's no great trick to cultivating a swamp in Florida.

Even the gators were real. They came from a nearby gator farm. They were harmless old daddies who were used to being around people. All they wanted to do was sleep in the sun and wait for some kind man to bring them their food.

I suppose that's why they were all riled now. They didn't know what to make of this outrageous man-size bundle of meat that had been dumped in their nice little sheltered swamp.

The tangle of gaudy, suffering foliage spread open on either side and my laboring boat *put-futted* into a jungle-ribbed slough. The water was as opaque as green milk-glass and there was a little setback in the mudbank on one side.

Three bewildered gators were standing there in the shallows grunting up. There wasn't much to them. The smallest was three foot and the largest six. Their manner seemed to imply that they didn't like the thing they had found in the water and why didn't someone come along and take it away because it obviously didn't belong there.

I idled the boat toward them and they lumbered off into the water in a tail-spanking huff. I had to get out of the boat and into the gafocky water up to my knees to get the body.

It was face down and it was a large man and when I rolled it over it was Robert Cochrane. A long knife was standing jauntily in the Irishman's chest right where people usually think the bull's-eye should be.

It had a mother-of-pearl handle.

Chapter Four

A fair crowd of Neverland employees had ganged around the dock and a couple of the uniformed lot guards were there making like FBI agents. They were the usual half-tough characters who always hold down jobs like that and they were having a swell time giving Freckles a pushing around when I got back with the boat and the body.

They lost interest in the scared kid. They damn near knocked each other into the water trying to get into the boat to have first look at the body.

"What a you know about this?" one of them growled at me.

Tough as nails. This was his big moment. Probably the only exciting thing that had happened to him all year was manhandling some poor drunk.

"I found him," I said.

"Jesus. I know that, I said—"

"That's all I know. I found him."

I was being a big help to him. He asked his partner wasn't I a big help and then the other toughy had a go at me.

"What the hell business was it of yours to go running in there after him?"

"The kid wasn't making much sense," I explained. "I thought maybe the gators were doing something to him."

"You know who shived him?" the first one asked me.

I shook my head and said, "Who killed Cock Robin?"

They looked at me and one of them said *Hmm?*

"Just a crazy association of ideas," I said. "Robert Cochrane, Cochrane Robert, Cock Robin. See?"

The one who had said *Hmm* said it again. The other one looked like he was getting pretty hot.

"You some kind of nut, buster, or what?" he wanted to know.

A broad bluff-faced man in a two hundred dollar suit pushed through the crowd and started yelling at the guards.

"Who is it? Simpson! Who's been hurt?"

The guard named Simpson got up and told him it was the boss and that he was dead.

"Jesus, Mr. Franks, somebody knifed him! It's murder!"

This Mr. Franks tucked in his mouth till it looked like a zipped purse and his eyes snapped at Simpson and at Cochrane's body and at me. He gave me a double snap.

"Who the hell are you?" he demanded.

I got out of the boat and joined him on the dock.

"I found him," I said. "After the kid started to unhinge."

"But who *are* you?"

"Thaxton."

"Thaxton-shmaxton!" he said furiously. "What the hell are you doing here? I don't know you."

"Makes us even. Who the hell are you?" I didn't need any more emotion blown in my face that morning.

He gave me a look that should have stuck four inches out my back.

"I'm Franks," he said. "Mr. Cochrane's business manager."

"I'm Thaxton," I said. "Mr. Cochrane's prestidigitator. He hired me yesterday."

"Thanks loads for the news," he said in a sour voice. He brushed by me like I wasn't somewhat in his way and got into the boat to have a look for himself.

Neverland didn't open till ten in the morning and it was now about eight-fourty. I wondered if they would open at all that day, and then I figured yes they would if May had her say. She could no more turn back a mark with a buck than a wolverine could refuse a dead rabbit.

I looked at the press of faces in front of me. I knew one of them. Billie. She was staring into the boat with a sort of entranced expression. I thought she was turning sick without realizing it. You could see that good-god knife in Cochrane real easy when one of the guards or Franks wasn't hunkering in front of him.

The law would arrive shortly and that would mean more tough talk in my face. I was in no hurry for it. I went over and got Billie by the elbow and said let's take a walk.

She looked up at me with a start and for a moment I don't think she knew who I was. Then she said Oh and bobbed her head. We pushed out of the goggling employees and started to walk, anywhere. It didn't matter what direction we took.

I felt a little like Alice in Wonderland. That's the way Neverland struck me when there weren't any people around. And right now there wasn't a soul. The marks wouldn't mob in till ten and the earlybird employees who were already on the lot were all over at the Swamp Ride or making for there as fast as their little feet could carry them.

"How did you happen to be there?" Billie asked me.

"I spent the night in Tarzan's hut," I told her. "But damned if Jane ever showed up. I think Cheeta did, though."

I glanced back at the looming, joined trees. Then I looked again. There was something monkey- or ape-like away up there in the midbranches. It stood out against the sky like a fly caught in a web.

"Look," I said. "Am I seeing things?"

She looked up over her shoulder and smiled.

"It's Terry Orme. He's Cheeta."

I said, "Huh?"

"He's a midget," Billie explained. "Rob Cochrane hired him to dress up in an apesuit and make like Cheeta. Until you get real close to him you'd swear it was an ape. The suit is a work of art and Terry acts more ape than human. I mean he can really climb."

I thought about it for a moment.

"Does he sleep up there at night?" I asked.

"Uh-huh. Funny little guy. He shies away from people."

Then I hadn't dreamed up Cheeta last night. I looked back at the tree again. The little apeman was still hanging there in the sky, staring down at the employees and at the boat that contained the employees' dead boss. He reminded me of Quasimodo brooding over the stupid populace of Paris from the high, gargoyled ramparts of Notre Dame.

We strolled through Pioneer Town and without people

around the place was like an old frontier ghost town, only it was in better shape than most ghost towns. I liked it that way. I could do without the people. I put my arm through Billie's arm. We hadn't said anything for a while.

We strolled down to a manmade lake complete with ducks and gliding swans. An island with real pine trees was out in the middle of it and an old fashioned high-pooped schooner was moored alongside the island. A big sign over the dock on the mainland said TREASURE ISLAND. The ticket-seller's stand was a window set in the side of a small old English structure that looked like a seaman's tavern. The warped signboard over the door said ADMIRAL BENBOW TEAROOM.

My interest perked up.

"Does that ship happen to be called the *Hispaniola?*" I asked.

"Yes. How did you know?"

"I'm a nut on *Treasure Island*. It was the first book I ever read and for year nothing could convince me that a better book had ever been written. Let's go over, huh?"

Billie gave me a funny little look.

"I'm beginning to understand you for the first time Thax" she said. "And I think I like you better for it."

"Me? What do you understand about me now that you didn't understand yesterday?"

"That your pseudo-tough don't-give-a-damn manner is an act. You're just a big-boned man who never quite grew up."

"Sure," I said. "Me and Peter Pan. That's how come I ended up in Neverland."

I didn't want to talk about the side of me that had never grown up. Embarrassed by being caught out, I guess. But it was true, in a way. Ever since I was a kid it has amazed me how most people in this godawful world think there is enough in their puny little mundane lives that they don't have to enhance it by escaping the brown-drab boredom of the present through books.

Life was a monotonous pain in the ass to me. And so were most of the people who comprised that life. Give me a good book by Kenneth Roberts or Walter D. Edmonds or Nordhoff and Hall and I can get to hell away from it. From the people too. I was a Then person. I didn't belong to the Now people.

What worried me right at that moment was the feeling that Billie was in the Nows' camp.

A school of rowboats was tied to the dock for the marks to rent and I handed Billie into one of them and shoved off and shipped the oar. She was still watching me with that funny little look.

"Cut it out," I said. "Every one of us is a nut someway or another."

"But you're a very special kind of nut, Thax. Because you don't fit in."

"Sure I do. Well enough to get by on."

Billie looked at the green duck-dirtied water overboard.

"Do you know what I was willing to do to get my first job in a carny?" she said. Her voice was very quiet.

"Cut it out."

"The owner was a Greek. A very fat, greasy Greek of fifty."

"I said cut it out."

She looked at me.

"But I wanted the job—a start—that bad," she said.

"All right," I said and I was goddam mad about it. "Now you've told me how you had to lay with a sweaty Greek who was old enough to be your grandpa in order to get your start. So now you're happy."

"I didn't say I was happy."

"Well it doesn't really matter, does it?"

She sighed. "That's my whole point. That's what you said yesterday when I said I hoped you'd get this job. It didn't really matter. That's the exact difference between us. It *does* matter."

"How?" I wanted to know. "Look. A hundred years from now there's going to be another poor mixed up sonofabitch just like me bumbling around on this earth. What am I going to mean to him then—or to anybody or anything?"

"I don't give a damn about a hundred years from now or ten thousand years!" she said urgently. "*We're* here now. You and I. It's our turn. And they're never going to give us a second shot at it."

I said nothing. I rowed the boat.

"Don't you see?" she said. "We've got to make the most of it. They start our kind out with nothing and if we slob around saying it doesn't really matter, then that's what we end up with. Nothing. Nowhere. I can't settle for that."

I beached the boat on Treasure Island and I got out and gave her a hand out. Then, as long as I had ahold of her and there was nobody else around and because I still didn't know what to say, I started to pull her in to me.

"No, Thax," she said.

"Why not?"

"Because I'm not sure yet. And I'm getting to an age where I've got to be sure."

"Because you're afraid of wasting your time on a bum huh?"

"Something like that," she said levelly. "And right, say it. I'm a bitch. A stupid little bitch with a dollar sign for a brain."

"I don't believe that any more than you do."

"Well," she said, "I don't like myself much when I talk like that, but sometimes I have to remind myself that I have a dream."

"Of what?"

"Of a better way to live. A very much better way."

I started to say it didn't really matter, but I didn't. I drew her in and I kissed her and her response was good but I didn't make with the hungry hands. I let her go.

She didn't say anything for a moment. She didn't look at me. Then she said, "We'd better get back."

I didn't like the idea at all but unless I resorted to rape what could I do? I said, "All right."

We didn't talk as I rowed us back to the dock.

Chapter Five

The luckboy who had sicked Eddy the pickpocket on me last night was strolling by the Admiral Benbow when we arrived at the dock. He grinned at me and called:

"How was it on the island?"

"The same as it is anywhere." I wasn't in the mood for fun and games and I guess it showed in my face or in my voice.

"Don't," Billie said to me. "Jerry's all right."

The lawyer-looking thief called Jerry laughed.

"That's what all the girls say," he said and winked at me. "Jerry's all right."

I had to smile. He was a friend of mine.

"I'll bet they do. How are things law-wise?"

"Booming. Simply booming. They've set up a sort of halfassed police station in the Okefenokee Arcade and the usual interrogation of anybody and everybody is well underway. I get it they'd like for you to show up for a minute or two." Jerry grinned again.

"Just the facts, mam. Just the grisly routine facts."

Billie looked up at me.

"Should I go with you, Thax?"

"Uh-uh. Why get involved? Go get ready for your show." I turned back to Jerry.

"The law going to let us open?"

"Sure. Everything but the Swamp Ride. Lieutenant Ferris, the dick in charge, was set to hold us closed. But Madame Cee came along and changed his mind for him." Jerry didn't wink again.

I figured he meant May when he said Madame Cee. I looked at Billie. There was nothing else to say. Not with Jerry the kid with the ears standing there.

"I'll see you later, Thax," she said.

I liked the way she looked at me when she said it. I said, "Sure. See you." Then I watched her walk away and it was something to look at—the way she handled that stern action. Jerry thought so too.

"Yeah," he said softly, his eyes following her.

I gave him an easy one in the ribs.

"Mine," I said. He looked at me, ready to smile.

"Think so?"

"I hope so," I told him. "C'mon."

I liked this Lieutenant Ferris right off. He was an old-time dick. I don't mean he was a daddy graybeard. I mean he looked like those violent men who came out of Prohibition and the Depression—the ones with the iron-eyed faces that might have belonged on either side of the law but couldn't possibly belong to any other strata of society. He was about fifty. A tired fifty.

"Sit anywhere," he told me.

There wasn't anywhere to sit, which didn't bother him because he was a stroller. He kept his hands in his pockets and his eyes on the floor and he strolled up and down while he talked. I pushed some cheap souvenir doodads to one side and parked myself on a counter.

"Name?"

"Thaxton." He glanced at me. "Well, are you going to add to that or just let it sit there?"

"L. M. Thaxton."

"I'm still waiting."

"Leslie Thaxton for crysake."

He grinned. "You were right the first time." He dropped his grin with a bang. "How come you got into the act this morning?"

I told him about me and the tree house and about Freckles yelling down the roof.

"So you decided to be a big help and go in there and haul the stiff all over the Swamp Ride. Anybody ever mention to you you ain't supposed to touch anything till the law arrives?"

"The kid was pretty hysterical. I didn't know but what those gators were eating somebody alive."

"Not those gators. The bigshot, Lloyd Franks, tells me they're as safe as housepets."

"I didn't know that," I said. "I only walked on the lot yesterday."

Ferris strolled away from me, four paces and turn and four paces back, watching the floor.

"What was the kid doing out there at that time of morning?"

"Part of his job, I suppose. Don't tell me you haven't questioned him yet?"

He took his eyes off the deck to give me an ironic look.

"You don't mind, do you, if we cross-examine his story?" Then he shrugged and took off on another short stroll.

"Yeah," he admitted, "the kid says it was his turn to show up early and try out the boats. Seems they do it every morning. That's one of the things that has me all ga-ga about this deal."

"What is?"

"Dumping Cochrane in there. I can't see any motive for

it. He was killed by the shiv about two AM. He wouldn't be in there taking the Swamp Ride at that time of night, would he? No. So it follows he was killed somewhere else on this lot. So why haul the body in there? The gator wouldn't touch it, and the whole damn place ain't deep enough to hide a dead rat in."

"You mean the murderer must have known the body would be found right away in the Swamp Ride, so why not leave it where he had killed it?"

"Yeah. And here's another thing. How did he get it in there? You can't handle any of those swamp boats without power. And if the murderer had used one of them, somebody around here would have heard the motor." He turned and looked at me.

"You for instance. You were sleeping right over the boats."

"Never heard a thing," I told him. "Slept like a baby."

Except for that time I thought I dreamed Cheeta came home, I thought. What had that little monkey Orme been up to?

A tough-faced harnessbull clomped into the arcade and handed Ferris a shoebox and a few grumbled words I couldn't catch. It must not have been big news to Ferris because he didn't start doing handsprings over it. He grunted and said okay and the storm trooper gave me a dirty look and clomped away.

Ferris opened the shoebox and took out a knife that could only be the murder weapon and he studied it for a minute like he was reading a list of instructions on how to stab.

He strolled over to me to let me marvel at it too.

"Recognize it?" he asked.

"I would if it was sticking in Cochrane's chest again."

"I mean do you recognize this *kind* of knife?"

"Um. Knife-thrower's. Perfect balance."

"Know who owns this particular one?"

I grinned at him. "The law does now. Before that I couldn't say. Might be anybody."

"Yeah. And whoever the anybody was he wore gloves. No prints. Unless—"His eyes took a stroll over me—"you wiped 'em off before you brought the body back to the dock."

"Try again," I suggested. "This whole deal doesn't mean a damn to me. I just work here. I'm not trying to cover up for anybody."

He waggled the blade absently, wearing a bemused expression.

"Is there a knife-throwing act on this lot?"

I was glad he phrased it that way. I wouldn't have to lie to him—unless you call an omission a lie.

"Not that I know of. But then I just—"

"Yeah, I know. You told me. You just started here." He looked sour for a minute. Then he grunted and almost smiled.

"You picked a hell of a swell time, didn't you?"

There was something in what he said, but it was too vague right then to mean anything. The timing was almost too coincidental.

"Well," I said, "it doesn't really matter, does it?"

I slid off the counter and told Ferris I had to see a man about my job. He didn't seem to care. I think he had already lost interest in me. When he told me to stick around in case he needed me, it sounded like he was saying it out of habit. I hoped so. I wanted a wide gap between myself and the law.

"Good luck," I told him. That was from habit too.

"Yeah," he said. The word didn't carry much conviction.

When I looked back he was still standing alone in the arcade, staring stonily at the floor.

Gabby had a stand set up for me. It was next door to Bill Duffy's bally platform. That was nice. Just a couple of old carny buddies working side by side. We looked at each other and looked away.

A shelf had been rigged behind my stand and it contained a vivid white orchid display.

"What's that for?" I asked Gabby. "I haven't turned pansy since you saw me last."

"The boss don't allow cash for cash gambling," Gabby told me. "We let the marks win an orchid. You're just here for the atmosphere. Didn't Rob explain that to you?"

"Yeah. But it only costs the mark a quarter a try. That's some deal, twobits for an orchid."

"Naw. These here are what they call saprophytic orchids. Don't have much value except for botanical purposes. Big old swamp a couple miles from here and the damn things grow wild in there by the million. Rob hires a kid to collect 'em. They're a dime a dozen."

"Just like barkers," I said.

"How'sit?"

"Something Cochrane said to me last night."

A dull look came into Gabby's morose face.

"I'm gonna miss that old Irish bastard," he said quietly.

"A pretty good guy, wasn't he?"

"The best."

"Evidently somebody around here didn't think so," I said. "Who do you think had it in for him?"

Gabby gave me a challenging look.

"Who do you think for godsake?"

"Hell, I don't know. I just started here, remember?

"Come off it, Thax. I know about you and May. Word gets around."

"That's what everybody keeps telling me." I looked over at Bill Duff. He was up on his baly spieling.

"Duff's big mouth has been going, huh?"

Gabby shrugged. "Did I say so?"

"You didn't have to. Well, it doesn't matter. Let's back up a couple of sentences. So you know me and May. So what?"

"So I know what everybody else around here knows. She was a knife-thrower when she first came to this lot. Before she put the hooks in Rob and became Mrs. Big."

I was surprised when he said that much. As a rule carny people never show any interest in a crime that happens in their backyard.They become deaf and dumb. They pointedly keep their noses out of it and volunteer nothing. It's the law's worry, not theirs. And Gabby was not a talkative man.

"You don't like May much, huh?" I prompted.

"Name me somebody here that does."

"Cochrane must have."

"Rob was easy. He liked everyone. He was a pushover for her."

"So now this word that gets around so fast has it that May turned the trick, huh?"

Gabby made a noise in his throat. "She's a cinch for it."

Could be. But what did it mean to me—except that I didn't like May and had liked her husband? It still wasn't any of my business. I just worked there. That was all.

Gabby took me around back to a little tented area and handed me my working togs—the flowered vest, the plastic bow tie, the derby and bally stick, and a final admonition.

"Remember, Thax. Atmosphere only. Don't send away any sore loser. May can afford the orchids."

That's right, I thought. It's May now. The whole kit and caboodle belongs to the little girl who came from the she house on D Street.

"I'll work out a routine," I promised him.

I arranged the three walnut shells and the little ivory pea just so and made a couple of practice passes to see if my hand was still in. The shell game has long been abandoned in favor of more ingenious and less discreditable methods of robbery, but it still holds a certain degree of fascination for today's so-called sophisticated marks. I started drumming up trade.

"Here we are, ladies and gentlemen! Carnival croquet, the preacher's pastime. Who'll risk a quarter to win an orchid? A *bee*-utiful laelia flower shipped from the Brazilian jungles at great expense to the management."

I grinned at the marks to show them I was just kidding.

"Step up and take a trip on the rolling ivory. It's a healthy sport, a clean game it's good for young and old! A child can understand it."

The marks were starting to gather. I gave them a free treat and made three passes with the shells, so rapid that even a missile-tracker couldn't have figured out where in hell that pea was.

The girls giggled and the young men grinned and hated my guts while they were grinning. You see a real pro do something that you couldn't hope to do in a million years and it's natural you should hate him even if you admire him. Especially if your girl is with you. Fall on your face, you showoff bastard, you silently pray.

"Gimme a quarter, hon," a cute little thing said to her boyfriend.

I smiled at the cute little thing and made a slow pass—left over right and middle under left and finished a figure eight. Sightless Sam could have followed the pass. The cute little thing didn't. She unerringly chose an empty. I had to thumb my spare pea into it to help her win.

"The little lady wins and the gambler loses," I announced and I handed her an orchid. "Now then, we're off on another journey. Who'll ride with me this time?"

I always let them win, sooner or later. Every so often a smart ass would give me some lip service and I'd hit him for sixbits before I'd donate an orchid to his girl. Working a shell game for fun can get to be a drag after a while, but it was good practice. And what the hell, it was a job.

"Three walnut igloos and an educated pill! Here we go again. Shoot a quarter, men, and win your girl or wife or secretary a priceless oncidium orchid straight from the wilds of the West Indies. A mere quarter. The fourth part of an overtaxed dollar."

There was a blonde thing who looked like she would have trouble spelling cat, and she thought I was the nuts. Every time I'd make a mildly naughty remark she'd come unstitched with the giggles. Her boyfriend was a sailor and he didn't think I was the nuts at all.

"We got a guy aboard ship who can do that better," he said in a quarterdeck voice. "All you need to beat him is a good eye."

It might cost me my job but it was worth it.

"Step aside, folks," I said. "Let the sailor see the pea." Barnacle Bill rolled up and gave me a one-cornered smirk.

"Go ahead," he said. "Shove 'em around."

I showed him the pea. I placed it under the middle shell. I shoved them around. His eyes followed like magnets.

"Slower," he ordered. "Like you do it for the bitches."

That sailorboy was simply begging for it. I raised one of the shells and let him see the pea again, and then I made a nice slow figure-eight pass. I practically had a signpost on the pea shell.

Quick as a wink he tapped the right one. I took the shell between my thumb and forefinger and made an imperceptible forward motion as I turned it over and palmed the little pea betweeen my third and fourth finger.

Popeye the sailor man stared at the empty shell.

"Every now and then the gambler wins a little," I said as I placed his quarter in my vest.

"You palmed it," he said, real mean.

I said nothing. I placed the empty shell down on the board and opened my hand, widespread. With my other hand I raised the far right shell and let him gaze at the pea.

"Around and around it goes, where it stops God only knows. Just an innocent little ivory ballbearing, friends. But it needs oil. Who's next to grease it or fleece it with a quarter?"

A goodnatured Pa-type mark started to make with a coin, but the sailor wasn't having any of that. He elbowed the Pa aside.

"Let's try that again." A very deadly Alan Ladd voice.

"You've forgotten something, haven't you, brother?" I suggested. I was egging him to grandstand. He did. He tossed a five dollar bill on the board.

"Match it."

I pretended I was stupid. "I'll have to give you your four seventyfive in quarters, friend."

"I didn't say nothing about change. I said match it."

I leaned over the board to confide in him.

"Sorry. This is only a quarter game. I'm not supposed to—"

"No guts, huh?" he sneered.

I pretended to think about it. "Very well, sir. If these other good people have no objection we'll call it an off the record sidebet. One Abe Lincoln it is."

I showed him the pea. I covered it. I made a pass like molasses in January. His eyes rode on the correct shell from beginning to end. Quick as a shot he covered the shell with a protecting palm. I looked at him. He grinned at me.

"This one," he said.

"Well, well," I said. "The groans of the gambler is sweet music in the winner's ear."

"Ain't it though?" He was getting a big kick out of my discomfort. "Care to double up?"

"No. I don't think I'd better."

"No," he sneered, "I didn't think you would. Better start counting out five bucks in quarters."

He turned the shell over. I didn't have to look to see that it was empty. I'd made sure of that before I let him cover it with his hand.

"Every now and then the gambler wins a little," I said as I gravely pocketed his five. Then I handed the giggly, placid-faced blonde an orchid. "Compliments of the management," I said.

The sailor was about to make something out of it, but I gave one of the lot guards the highsign and he came over and took care of it. During a lull Bill Duff stepped down from his bally stand and strolled over to see me.

"Hello, Bill." I didn't work up much enthusiasm.

He said, "Thax." Then he said, "You'll lose your job real quick if somebody registers a bitch about that little trick you just turned. Cash for cash gambling's taboo around here. You're supposed to work on wages, not on take."

"Good old Bill" I said. "Always sticking your beak in my business. No, on second thought I guess it wasn't your beak you stuck in. Or was it?"

Bill started to get red. "I'm just telling you is all. That old-time reaming don't go here. Old man Cochrane won't . . ." He stopped. I guess he just remembered that old man Cochrane no longer had a thing to say about Neverland.

"That was yesterday, Bill," I said. "Today all I have to do to square it is tip May fifty percent of the take."

Duff shook his head at me as if he couldn't understand how anyone as simple-minded as I appeared to be could go around without a keeper.

"You never did understand May, Thax. Lived with her for what was it—six years? And still you thought all she was after was the buck. When that wasn't it at all."

"Naw, naw. Not May. May's all heart. All out for her friends. Anybody knows that. Just ask 'em."

"Go ahead and laugh, Thax, you know so goddam much. But I'll say this for May—she offered me a hand when I showed up here down on my luck."

Which shows how much Duff knew about May and Robert Cochrane.

"Yes," I said, "I can't deny she was good to you, Bill. You've certainly made a big success of it."

He looked puzzled and then he started to get mad, but I

had already spotted Billie heading for the nautch show and I dodged around the stand and went after her.

"Billie."

She looked back and saw me and smiled and came to a stop.

"Hi, Thax."

Funny thing. Standing there in the middle of Neverland with hundreds of loud-mouthed people milling around us, it still seemed like we were alone in a little world all of our own. Falling in love does that to you. It seems to surround you and the one you love in a shimmering crystal ball. The millions of people outside the ball are all mundane nonentities.

If a newsboy were to rush by right then yelling "Russia declares war on U.S.!" I couldn't have cared less. Just Billie. That's all there was.

"How are you making out?" she asked me.

"All right. It's a job."

"Did the police give you a bad time?"

"No." I kept staring at her.

"Don't do that, Thax. There's people around."

"Do what?"

"Look at me that way. You look like you wanted to eat me alive."

"I've already considered that."

"Oh honestly, Thax. What's wrong with you?" She wasn't really mad. I grinned at her.

"You going to work now?"

"Yes."

"How about meeting me tonight?"

A little V of consternation formed in her brows.

"I can't, Thax. Really. I've got something on tonight."

Another funny thing—the way instant jealousy can go off in a man like a hand grenade when he hardly even knows the girl who has perhaps just caught his eye.

"Date?" I said.

"Thax." Her voice was low, appealing. "Don't look like *that* either. No it isn't a date. It's just something personal I have to do. Alone. Some paperwork."

"Like a college girl with her term paper," I said.

Her laugh sounded a little embarrassed.

"I barely got through the eleventh grade, Thax."

"You're one up on me" I told her. I didn't tell her about Miss Raye who had been my tenth grade Lit teacher and who had thought I was very sensitive and used to have me over to her apartment after school to discuss books and writers and something else, until her landlady found out about it (I mean the something else) and told the school and they told my parents and then everything became very messy because I was only sixteen and Miss Raye was thirty-eight. And so I never did finish the tenth grade—though I've always felt that what I learned from Miss Raye was mighty valuable instruction in any man's education.

"Well," I said. "See you tomorrow then."

"All right, Thax. Tomorrow."

She reached and touched my hand.

"Not mad? I mean about tonight?"

"Uh-uh. Just suicide sick with disappointment."

"Thax," she said.

We smiled at each other and I said, "All right, I'll fight it. Have I told you the old Thaxton battle cry? 'Can Thaxtons fight? Aye, through the day and all the night!' "

Billie laughed. "The last time I heard that it was in Robert Taylor's *Ivanhoe* movie. Only then it was 'Can *Saxons* fight.' "

I shrugged. "Borrow a little here, steal a little there."

She said, "I'll see you later, Thax," and I said, "Sure. See you." And again I watched her walk off with all that hind action, and for a very wild and vivid moment I felt like a frustrated he dog when the bitch next door was in heat.

Then it passed, more or less, and I went back to work.

Chapter Six

Cheeta swung into Tarzan's tree house that night—through the window and into his bed. It was Terry Orme, the apeman.

I struck a match and we looked at each other. I had been sitting there in the dark waiting to see if he would show up.

"I'm your roomy," I told him. "My name is Thax."

He didn't say anything. He studied me until the match

began to hurt and I put it out. Then he spoke.

"There's a Coleman under that bed." His voice was like his body, a pipy little thing.

I rummaged under the zebra-clad bed and found the lantern and struck another match and ignited the two suspended bags in the lamp. A Coleman is brighter than the average lightbulb but it can throw weird shadows. Terry Orme looked a little weird sitting across the wide African room from me. He wasn't but about forty inches high.

I always think of midgets as being those poor little bastards with the large heads and the stunted arms and legs—which isn't so, because a true midget has a perfectly proportioned body, and they are a rare species.

I suppose that's why Terry Orme reminded me more of a jockey than of a midget. There was nothing foreshortened about his limbs: he was just very small. I couldn't even make a stab at guessing his age.

"You always come in through windows?" I asked him.

"You mind?" Tough little cuss.

Uh-uh. I'm really working around to ask how come you're out climbing trees at this time of night?"

"How long have you had nose trouble?" he shot back. Some jockey.

I got up and walked over to him and he sort of hunched back on his little bed. I suppose I looked like a giant to him. And when you think of it, that's a hell of a way to go through life—living in a world where all the people around you are belt buckles.

How would you like to go swimming at the beach and have to look eye to eye with all the girls' navels?

I put out my hand.

"If we're going to be roomies, Orme, why not be friends?"

He looked at my hamsized hand but didn't take it. His small face was sullen.

"I don't have any friends."

I hung in there. I could be just as stubborn.

"You got me, Terry. All it costs is a smile." I thrust my hand closer.

"Well—" he muttered. Then he shook.

I smiled and went back and sat on my bed and gave

myself a smoke. If I had him pegged right all I had to do was keep quiet and he'd emerge on his own. Because now it was his turn to make with the overtures.

He scowled at the floor and sent me a couple of covert glances.

"I got enough geetus that I don't have to live up here if I don't want," he said all at once. "I stay by myself because I don't like people. Most of 'em, anyhow."

"Same with me. You ever hear what Remarque said about that?"

"Who the hell's Remarque?" He couldn't growl in his pipy voice but he tried.

"Erich Maria Remarque. The guy who wrote *All Quiet on the Western Front*. These two guys are in a bar, see? One says to the other, 'You like Americans?' the other guy says, 'No.' 'You like Englishmen?' the first asks. 'No.' 'Germans?' 'No.' 'Spaniards?' 'No.' 'Frenchmen?' 'No.' The first guy gets POed. 'Well, who in hell do you like?' And right away the other guy says, 'I like my friends.' "

Terry Orme smiled, a little, and said, "I guess that about covers it." He looked at me. "You must read a lot, huh?"

"Now you're talking about man's best friend. A good book will never let you down no matter how often you go back to it."

He looked down at his little hands.

"You'd get along with Mike Ransome," he said.

"He read a lot?"

"Yeah." Terry hopped down from his bed and started to pace across the leopardskin rug.

"What's Ransome's job?" I asked, but he didn't seem to hear me.

All three foot four of him stalked back and stopped in front of me. Something was bugging him bad. I don't mean just his natural frustration over being a freak. A kind of enigmatic anger and fear kept playing over his face like a little girl jumping rope.

"The marks watch me scramble around in that apesuit and they think I'm a real monkey," he said. "But as far as I'm concerned I'm making a monkey out of them."

I nodded. I figured he would look at it that way. It gave him a slice of superiority. God knows he needed it.

"I wouldn't have this job if I didn't like it." He was getting defiant now. Defiance for defense.

"I like climbing around. You see and hear things. Things you'd never dream of."

The little warped soul was climbing out of the cracked shell. He was growing bigger in his own eyes all the time. Society had put him down all his life, had looked at him and grinned and said "Look at the freak." He got back at them by spying on their tawdry secrets. Come right down to it, the poor little bastard was probably nothing more than a frustrated Peeping Tom.

"Is that what you were doing tonight?" I wondered.

He said yeah. Then he seemed to shrink inside himself again. He went back to his little bed and climbed up on it like a child.

"The law has taken over the bunkhouse for their headquarters," he told me. "That Ferris cop was in there going around and around with Franks a little while ago. Franks wants Ferris to give him the go-ahead on opening up the Swamp Ride again."

"But Ferris still wants to play Sam Spade in there, huh?"

"Yeah. And can you imagine the trade the lot's losing by keeping it closed? The marks are just panting to get in there and see the spot where old man Cochrane was found."

I was disgusted. "As a business manager that Franks is some shrewd cooky."

"It ain't Franks," Terry said. "He just does what May Cochrane tells him to. Everybody knows that."

I said, "Jesus." There were times when May made me want to throw up.

Terry was watching me with an odd look. I had an idea that the word that got around had reached him and he knew that I had once been married to May. He asked me something out of the blue.

"You getting soft on Billie Peeler?"

I wondered if Terry had a crush on Billie, in his hopeless little way. I said, "Uh-huh."

He looked at his little hands again. "She's a good kid. We worked together in K. C. a couple years back. She—"

There was a quiet knock of noise from somewhere outside the tree house, but close by. I glanced at Terry. He gave me a start. His delicately small face was frozen terror.

I didn't say anything. I got up and walked over to the open doorway and stepped onto the porch and looked around.

Most of the lights were off in Neverland and I couldn't see much for the maze of phony leaves and the shadows they cast. A single spot was blazing over the deserted Swamp Ride dock and it made the placid water look like cold splitpea soup. I didn't see any sign of movement.

"Who is it?" Terry's thin voice piped behind me. "Is it a guy or a girl?"

"Just a noise in the night, I guess," I called back. "I don't see anyone."

I didn't see anyone when I turned back into Tarzan's hut either. Terry Orme had vanished.

I took a rowboat back to Treasure Island the next morning before the lot opened. Silly I guess, but being out there by myself made me feel at home. If any marks or sweep-up men had been around they would have spoiled it for me. Then it would have been just another Neverland attraction.

I beached the boat a few yards astern of the *Hispaniola* and got out to look the little island over.

"Ah," I said, quoting Long John Silver. "This here is a sweet spot, this island. A sweet spot for a lad to get ashore on."

Funny, but that's how I felt—like a kid again.

They had done a very nice job with the layout. They had humped up three scrubby little dirt hills and each one had a skull-and-crossbones sign planted at its base: Mizzenmast Hill, Spyglass Hill and Foremast Hill. Then they had Flint's Stockade, where Jim Hawkins and Captain Smolett, Doctor Livesey and Squire Trelawney had held off Silver's cutthroats.

A sign reading *To Flint's Treasure Pit* pointed down a woody path and I followed it into a sunny glen. The Treasure Pit was at the foot of a hardwood ridge. It was a shallow hole in the ground with a spade and a broken pick stuck in the dirt, and a tangle of blocks and tackle and an old half-buried sea chest with the name *Walrus* on it.

That familiar atavistic feeling of being watched nudged

me and I turned around and looked at a little scrub rise a few yards away. I didn't see anything and I shrugged it off and started to turn back into the path.

A wildman leaped right through a palinetto screen and landed like an animal smack in front of me. Honest to God I nearly wet myself.

He had a wild mop of gray hair and a beard to match and he was dressed in old bits of sailcloth and skins that were held together by brass buttons and rawhide thongs.

He hunched and hunkered and giggled and scratched himself and made erratic gestures with his hands. He shuttled toward me crabwise. And damned if I didn't back off.

"Who the hell are you?" I nearly yelled it at him.

"I'm poor Ben Gunn, I am. And I haven't spoke with a Christian these three years."

I could have kicked myself. Of course they had to have a Ben Gunn on the island. They probably had a one-legged character making like Long John Silver too. I started to laugh.

"Man," I said. "I nearly dropped my load when you jumped out like that."

The actor chuckled and straightened out of character. He was about my tall but there wasn't much heft to him. He looked as wiry and agile as a young Italian acrobat.

"It gets 'em all," he said delightedly. "Especially the young stuff. I can make them leap halfway out of their panties."

"Let me know the next time you make one leap," I said. "They won't let me in the nautch show."

He laughed. "You're Thaxton, aren't you? The new chap with the hots for Billie?"

I looked at him. I wasn't sure how I wanted to take that.

He slapped me on the back.

"Just clowning, boy. Don't get sore. Billie's a good kid."

"That's what Terry Orme told me," I said. "Maybe I should start to wonder just how good Billie is."

"You know Terry?" He looked mildly surprised.

"We're roomies up in the tree house. He lives there because he doesn't like people around. I'm there because I'm tap city."

"No kidding," he said. "I never knew Terry bunked up

there." He smiled and shrugged. "Well, he's not the only screwball around here. I bunk aboard the *Hispaniola* myself. By the by, my name's Mike Ransome."

"Oh. The guy who reads a lot. Shake, brother."

"You too?" He looked pleased about it. "What do you think of R. L. S.?"

I stalled a moment to dredge up one of the lines from my subconscious. I worked with a telepathist once and it's amazing the tricks of memory you can pick up in a racket like that.

"Flint is dead," I misquoted. "But some of his hands are aboard, worse luck for the rest of us."

"Hey!" Mike cried. "A *Treasure Island* buff." He grabbed me by the arm. "C'mon, Thax. I want you to see my schooner."

He told me about Neverland's Treasure Island as we walked.

"It was all my idea. Old Cochrane went for it like a ton of bricks. Let me design the whole layout to suit myself. We take the marks aboard the *Hispaniola* over at the dock, see? Give'em a sail around the island and then we land 'em and divide'em into groups and give each group a treasure map. You know—that treasure hunt game kids play at parties? It works like that. Of course the actual treasure they finally find is only souvenirs, costume jewelry—junk like that—but it makes the marks happy."

He was as effusive as a kid about it. He practically skipped while we walked and he talked. I was beginning to wonder if he might be a trifle gay.

He trotted up the *Hispaniola's* gangplank like an overgrown Peter Pan, calling, "C'mon, Thax. I want you to see my cabin."

"I bet you do," I thought.

But he was all right. He didn't try any hankypanky. He pulled off his wig and beard and I could see that under the grease paint he was only about twentyfive.

He lived in the schooner's aft cabin. It was always kept locked off from the deck. That way the godawful scramble of marks couldn't pry into his home. I looked around and wondered what he used for a head. Probably the lake. There were three handy stern windows.

He had a table set into the butt of the mizzenmast and benches and a bunk bed over some lockers and the windows gave a nice light. He had bookshelves in the starboard wall. I skimmed over some of the titles. He really was a nut on Stevenson . . .

The Wrecker, The Dynamiter, Prince Otto, Merry Men, Kidnapped, David Balfour, Master of Ballantrae, six editions of *Treasure Island,* each illustrated by a different artist, and even a copy of *A Child's Garden of Verses.*

Mike Ransome was watching me, beaming like a kid.

"Know what I like about Stevenson?" he asked. "The deserving always find what they were searching for and live happily ever after. That's the way I like a story to end."

"Too bad life isn't like that," I said. "Stevenson was a romantic daydreamer. He believed in finding treasure. But who the hell says it follows you'll be happy for the rest of your life just because you stumbled on a treasure?"

"Well, Jim Hawkins lived happily ever after, didn't he?"

"I always like to think he did," I said. "But I've got my doubts. Anyhow, look at the protagonist in *Ebb Tide.* He didn't find his treasure."

"Not in pearls or pounds," Mike said. "But he found something better—at least better for him. Treasure, after all, is only a relative term. A loaf of bread can be a treasure to one man, and an idea can be a treasure to another. It's all in what you need."

He had me there and I admitted it.

"How about some music?" he said.

He had a hi-fi in there and he put on a record. It was a heavy-bodied instrumental and it throbbed mood through the cabin. I haven't much ear for music. I couldn't get too excited over it.

Mike heated a pot of coffee on a hotplate and we sat down at the table to talk and smoke. He drank his java black, cup after cup. He seemed to grow more effusive all the time. He damn near bubbled he was so effervescent. After a while he got on my nerves, a little.

"Well," I said, "this has been nice, but the marks are about due to arrive. I've got to get to my stand. Thanks for the jo." It was damn near floating my hind teeth.

Mike saw me to the door. He was back in character again, beard or not.

"When Ben Gunn is wanted, you know where to find him. Just where you found him today. And him that comes is to have a white thing in his hand and he's to come alone."

He even nipped me on the elbow, Gunn-style.

"Watch out for Darby M'Graw," I said. "I understand his ghost is somewhere on this island."

Mike laughed delightedly.

Halfway across the lake I looked up from my rowing and saw Mike Ransome. He had climbed the schooner's main shrouds and he was waving his wig and beard at me.

All it did for me was make me feel older than I was.

Chapter Seven

The storm trooper who had tipped me the dirty look in the arcade the day before was standing like a sentry in front of the Admiral Benbow door. He warned me away from the area with another dirty look.

I didn't give a damn. I didn't want any tea.

The luckboy Jerry fell in with me when I reached Pioneer Town. He looked very reserved and lawyerish, until he winked and showed me a pair of handcuffs.

"Off that john?" I asked. "Why, for godsake?"

"I don't like cops that are all fatassed with self-importance," Jerry said. "I was merely strolling by the tea-room and he says to me 'Keep moving, pimp.'" He shook his head emphatically.

"That's just begging for it, you know? I'll wait a bit, then I'll put Eddy on to his badge. Later on I'll put another boy on his Roscoe."

"Well, it doesn't matter to me," I said. "You can clean him down to his tobacco-stained shorts for all I care. But what's the big deal in the Admiral Benbow?"

"The law, my son," Jerry said in his judicial voice, "has blundered upon what is known in the jargon as a clue." He dropped the W. C. Fields manner and became himself.

"That's it, baby. They figure they've found X marks the spot where Cochrane got it."

"In the Admiral Benbow?"

"Yeah. They found a splotch of blood on the floor and it matches Cochrane's type. Nobody noticed it till last night because a teatable had been set over it. One of the rummies swamping out the joint found bingo after the lot closed at midnight."

"Huh," I said. "Just like Billy Bones."

Jerry looked at me. "How'sit?"

"Nothing," I said. "Just an association of ideas."

I had no sooner got my stand set up and had started my spiel when a handsome young plainclothes dick came at me like Mercury the god and said, "Mr. Thaxton?"

"Yeah?"

"Please come with me. Lieutenant Ferris wants to see you."

"What's the bitch now?"

The naughty word did not make a hit with him. He looked annoyed.

"Lieutenant Ferris will inform you in due time?"

Talk about an officious little snot—even if he was six-one. I made a pass with the walnut shells.

"Care to try your luck, son? Win a nice orchid for your little old mother?"

He drew himself up to a shade over six-one and said, "Mr. Thaxton, I'll have to ask you to accompany me without any nonsense."

I swept up my shells and pea and pocketed them.

"Shall I take your arm or will you take mine?" I asked. Then, with a polite little bow, I offered him back his wallet.

"You dropped this, I think. Mustn't lose it. It contains your little tin badge."

"I don't want to have to resort to force, sir," he said, stiff as starch. "It would be very embarrassing to both of us."

"You're right. I haven't been spanked in twenty years."

Bill Duff was all eyes over on his bally. He was probably hoping the law would let me have the book. I gave him the well-known finger salute and fell in with the New Breed type of dick.

Gabby edged down to one end of his counter and looked at me. Funny about carny people. If they're square they'll do anything for each other. All he was waiting for was a highsign from me. Then he would create some kind of phony commotion, to give me a running chance. I shook my head at him.

This new breeder didn't take me to the Admiral Benbow. He marched me to hell and gone beyond the Watusi Village to the bunkhouse. It wasn't much—a long, low, tarpaper shack with a row of surplus army cots and a table and and couple of benches. It had that sour rummy smell of stale booze and sweat and vomit.

Ferris was sitting on one side of the table. He looked at me and his eyes were as opaque as two paving stones.

"You goddam liar, Thaxton," he said.

I stared back at him for a count of three. Then I nodded at young Adonis.

"Will I have the boy from Yale on me too, if I go for you?"

"Just save the goddam tough talk for the tourists," Ferris snapped. "You ain't about to fight me or anybody. Sit down."

I sat down at the table. The young dick stood over me like an MP. Ferris didn't seem to like him much better than I did. It was hard to be yourself around a big self-righteous kid like that.

"All right, Larry," Ferris said to the stern youngster. "Wait outside, huh?"

The kid tramped away like a good soldier and I looked at Ferris.

"Some politician's son?" I suggested.

"Near enough," Ferris admitted in a grumble. "The DA's nephew. Jesus," he added.

"I think you called me a liar," I reminded him.

"You're goddam right I did, smart ass. We've done a little enquiring on the wire since I last talked to you. Why'd you hold back on me about you and Mrs. Cochrane?"

"A sin of omission isn't a lie," I said. "You didn't ask me about my past marital mistakes."

"Jesus," he said. "Carny people. Never volunteer anything, huh? Look, Thaxton. If you had admitted to me that she used to be your wife you could just as well have told me that she also used to be a pro knife-thrower. And you goddam well could have told me that the shiv we found in Cochrane was one of hers!"

I said nothing. I dug out a cigarette and rolled it between my fingers. Ferris thumbnailed a match and held it out to me.

"You aren't as simple-minded as you make out, Thaxton," he said. "What's the first thing a dick looks for in a murder case?"

I shrugged. "Motive?"

"Bet your sweet butt! First and last. And now here's another toughy for you. What one outstanding person has the motive in this case?"

"How would I know? Am I God?"

Ferris looked at me. He looked sick. He said Jesus again.

"Thaxton—be good to me, huh. I'm working for the city. I'm working on a salary for a pension. I have the commissioner and the DA on my back. I don't have all day to play patty-cake."

"Look," I said, "if you mean that May inherits the gold, say so. I don't know. I haven't been shown Cochrane's will."

"Well, I have!" He didn't quite shout it at me.

"What's wrong? Did he leave you out of it?"

Ferris ignored my funny. He hunched over the table. "Your ex-wife picks up the full packet. Got any idea what it's worth?"

"Should be a fair sized bundle."

"Yeah. I'll drop you a little hint. This place grossed thirty mill last year."

Now it was my turn to say it. "Jesus," I said.

"You like the motive? It catches your eye?"

"Eye, ear and nose too. Money has a nice smell. But that doesn't prove she killed him."

"Come on," he said. "Come on."

"No, I'm serious. Maybe she loved her husband."

"Ummm, sure. A cool, sexy article like that. And him only twentyfive years older than her. Sure, nuts about him."

"Well, maybe she simply liked him then. He was a likable guy."

"Why sweat it?" Ferris asked. "You can't ignore that knife. It was hers. And here's another little item for your consideration. My boys found a jade earring on the mudbank where Cochrane's body was. Guess who owns the matching earring."

"My ex-wife?"

"Your ex-wife. And another point. She was here on the lot the night he was murdered. She claims she was up in her suite asleep, but she has no witnesses."

"I should hope not," I said, but my mind was on something not so flippant. It looked bad for May. It had looked bad for her right from the time I found her knife in her husband. The thing was though, it was starting to look a little *too bad.* Or too much. And I got the feeling that maybe Ferris was thinking the same thing. He didn't really look as pleased with his case as he should have.

"It's a nice little case," I said.

He didn't say anything. He watched me with a somber expression. So I went on and said what I thought might be in both our minds.

"Beautiful, hard-hearted ex-knife-thrower marries kindly rich old coot. Whole world shakes its head knowingly. Gold digger strikes lush pocket. Everybody says so. Nobody likes bitchy wife except maybe rich old husband and a few young lovers. Rich old husband gets murdered with knife that so obviously belongs to gold-digging wife that it runs out and bites you in the leg to attract attention. Wife's jade earring is found near corpse. Wife was in locality at time of murder. Wife can't produce alibi."

I lit another cigarette. "Strike you the same way it does me?"

Ferris tucked in his mouth and looked unhappy.

"All right," he said. "So it has the smell of a frame."

"The framework is downright stinking when you start to push at it. Sure—as soon as I saw the body and the weapon I put two and two together and what they made wants to be the widow queen of Neverland. But then I had another look at that knife. The blow that killed Cochrane was a downward thrust. A knife-thrower strikes from a distance. He or she doesn't stab. True, a knife's a woman's weapon, but a woman will usually give it to you in the back, won't she. Cochrane was a pretty tough old Irishman. I don't think May could have stabbed him from the front, unless he'd been asleep, and then the angle's still wrong."

Ferris lit a cigarette. He said nothing.

"And here's another weak beam in the frame," I said. "Aside from the fact that there's no valid reason why the body should have been moved from the Admiral Benbow to the Swamp Ride—how the hell would a woman haul a big heavy body like that? Even if she had used one of those boats, how did she get the stiff from the tearoom to the Swamp Ride dock? And why in God's name would she leave that shiv in him when it practically stands up and shouts 'This murder weapon belongs to May Cochrane!' "

Ferris studied the ashy tip on his cigarette.

"Maybe she had help with moving the body."

I had an idea what was coming next. He looked at me.

"Funny," he said, "when you think about the timing. You show up, Cochrane gives you a job, you go see his wife—yeah, I know about your little visit with your ex-wife—and a few hours later Cochrane gets killed and your ex-wife ends up with the gold."

"If you'd checked back far enough," I said, "you'd have found out that May divorced me because she hated my guts. It was coincidence I ended up at her present husband's lot. It wasn't planned that way."

He didn't really want to smoke his cigarette. He mashed it out.

"I did check back far enough," he said quietly. "And I turned up an interesting little item with your name on it."

This time I damn well knew what was coming next. It was my little blue ribbon that followed me wherever I went.

"Teenage rape is a messy item in any man's language." His voice was casual, very casual. I let out my breath.

"All right," I said. "You want to hear what happened, or you just want to build a case against me out of a lot of five-year-old hysteria reports?"

"You tell me."

"This hot little thing used to come on the lot every night when I was spieling for my wife with Brody's carny," I told him. "When I say hot, I mean kayriced almighty she made you think of instant bedroom. She'd hang around my bally stand and give me the eye while I was making with the words. Whenever I'd have a lull, I'd shoot the breeze with her. You know, playful sex-talk that tells you whether you're going to be in or not. I was in.

"May and I hadn't been getting on for a couple of years. It had turned into a marriage in name only. In short, I wasn't getting my share. So I was ripe when this little sex-pot gave me a tumble. She went for me. Funny thing is, I went for her. I don't mean just her body. I liked her.

"We went to a hotel. Everything was fine. We went again. I think she was in love with me, or thought she was. I—"

"Back up a minute," Ferris interrupted. "You knew her age when you took her to the motel?"

"Let me tell it my way, huh? I like to do it story style. No, I didn't know her age. She told me she was nineteen and she looked it. But I figured her for eighteen just to be on the safe side. The truth was she was only seventeen and I was on the bad news side. But I didn't find it out until after the world turned over. You see, we had started to talk about me getting a divorce and us getting married." I blew my breath again.

"Then her old lady found out. Jesus. It was something. The old lady is having a screaming fit. The old man is trying to get at me with a stick. The local law is trying to hold him back and give me a roughing up at the same time. Brody is yelling he'll have me blacklisted on every lot in the land. My wife is calling me all the nice names she'd picked from her whory mother. The seventeen-year-old is bawling. Nobody will listen to me. Nobody will let me explain. I'm standing there like a bewildered asshole."

Ferris started to chuckle and I shook my head in disgust.

"God," I said. "So the seventeen-year-old panics. It's my fault, she says. I seduced her. I got her drunk. She did't know what she was doing. No, she didn't know I was married. No, I never had said anything about marrying her. Well—" I shrugged.

"So anyhow, her old lady was afraid of the scandal. Her brother was the mayor's brother-in-law or something like that, and the whole mess was covered up. Brody fired me, the law ran me out of the state, and my wife happily sued for divorce. End." I mashed out my cigarette.

"You were lucky, you know?" Ferris said. "Because the law says a seventeen-year-old girl *doesn't* know what she's doing and it damn well means rape."

I gave him a sick look. "Will you stop it?" I said. "Doesn't know what she's doing, shi—"

"No, I mean it. As long as she's under eighteen the entire blame goes up your chute. Even if she pulls off all her clothes and climbs in your bed and gives consent, the law still states she doesn't know what she's doing."

"All right. But it's a goddam stupid law and you know it. So don't look so self-righteous. You would have done just what I did, if you'd had the chance."

He cocked an eye. "Me? At my age?"

"Yes, you at your age. And you're probably happily married and have a couple of grown kids and you're a cop, and yet if a sexy little seventeen-year-old were to come waggling her behind in here and throw it at you, and if there was nobody around and you were damn well certain that you could get away with it—you'd do it. Any normal man would."

He thought about it for a moment and I could see the truth in his eyes. Any man.

"Well," he said, "I guess that's why they made the law."

"I guess," I said. "Look, before we started with the saga of my sex life, you were trying to make me think that you thought I had something to do with Cochrane's death."

"Did you?"

"Kind of silly supposition, isn't it? I mean when you think about it? My ex-wife says to me 'Help me knock off my hubby and I'll inherit the bundle and give you halvies.' So to prove my brilliance of mind I take one of her special knives and I kill the old gentleman and put him where half the world will see him the first thing in the morning, and then—just to make certain everybody will know my ex-wife had a hand in it—I leave one of her earrings with the body. That way she's bound to get caught, and she'll squeal on me, and I'll end up with nothing but a free ticket on the electric chair ride."

"It's just possible that your ex-wife had nothing to do with this murder," Ferris said in his casual voice.

"I take it you're working on a brand new supposition. I'm listening avidly with all three ears."

"It's just possible the motive wasn't money."

"Meaning?"

"Revenge."

"Oh," I said. "I can put up my hand now. I know the answer to that one. Me. *My* revenge against my bitchy ex-wife. I'm down and out. I come here and get a twobit job from Cochrane. I discover that his wife is my ex-wife who once raked me over the coals. Now she's sitting on a bundle of greenbacks and I don't have a pot to pit in. I'm jealous. I go mad. I knife the old gentleman and frame it around my ex-wife. I'm happy. I live happily ever after spieling for the spider lady in the sideshow. Something like that, huh?"

Ferris grinned at me. "Something like it, yeah."

He got up to take a stroll around the room. I'd been wondering when he was going to start that. But then this case was slowing him down physically. He'd been staying up nights working out suppositions. He wandered back to the table, looking at me.

"You'll admit it has possibilities?" His manner was politely inquiring, but I could damn near hear the wheels go round in his head. He had given the possibility some heavy thought.

"Bet your butt it does," I said. "And I'll give you another butt-betting possibility. It's name is Bill Duff."

In an earlier context I mentioned that carny people clam up when a crime is committed in their territory. But I didn't mind sicking the law on Duff. I loved him like he loved me. And a rather obvious possibility had just crossed my mind. Maybe Ferris hadn't made his inquiries on the wire. Maybe Bill Duff—that snide sonofabitch—had put him wise about my past.

Ferris nodded. "I'm still giving that one some consideration. We know that this Duff and your ex-wife used to be like that." He crossed his index over his forefinger to show me.

"That's Duff on the bottom." I pointed at his lower finger. "May always liked it that way."

Ferris actually laughed.

"Thaxton, you have a dirty dirty mind. Get the hell out of here now, huh? I've got other people to see."

I got out of there. When I looked back through the screen-door Ferris was doing what he had done the last time I'd walked away from him—standing still and staring at the floor? But I had the feeling that this time he was thinking about me.

Chapter Eight

One of those cute little highschool things in the red-and-white guide outfit came up to me with a nice clean smile. This one wore a very short skirt and she had pretty legs. I wondered if she was seventeen.

"Pardon me, sir, but aren't you Mr.Thaxton?"

I admitted I was as I ran my eye from the tip of her toes to the top of her hose. Which I couldn't actually see because it disappeared under her skimpy skirt. Which was just about as high as the law would allow in public. Any higher and the vice squad would slap a morals charge on the Cochrane Enterprises.

Nix, nix, I told myself. She looks seventeen, she'll claim eighteen, and tomorrow morning her battle-ax mama will rush in yelling she's only sixteen. But I was only kidding myself. I didn't really care. Not too much.

"Mr.Franks has been looking everywhere for you, sir," she said with the nice clean smile that was starting to get on my nerves. Whatever happened to all the whory looking, hard-eyed tarts who used to haunt carny lots?

"For me? Why?"

"I'm sure I don't know, sir. He simply said—"

I'd been through this same dialogue with one of her nice clean boyfriends. "Okay, okay. Where does he want to see me?"

She didn't quite point because anybody knows that's bad manners, but made a sort of indicative gesture toward the south.

"His office is upstairs over the storerooms, sir."

Upstairs, naturally. With Private on the door. I smiled at the bright little thing and looped my arm in hers.

"Show me, huh?"

You'd have thought I had pinched her where I shouldn't.

"Please, Mr Thaxton! That sort of familiarity isn't necessary."

I decided she was a little college thing. They usually don't know a term like familiarity in highschool. That was my top-o-the-head thought. My sub-level thought was more basic, more home-truthish. It was this:

You're dated, boy. You're age-lagging. Once past thirty you enter the anachronism stage. The young tasties are starting to think of you as Uncle Thax.

You want the truth? It hurt when she backed off from me. That's a funny and goddam tragic thing about a man. No matter how old or how wise he becomes he still needs to feel that every good-looking female between fifteen and fifty is instantly attracted by his magnetic personality. When they aren't—he dies.

"Forgive me," I said with a bitter smile (bitterness usually rouses the inate sympathy in a female). "Now and then I encounter an honest to God virgin and I forget how to act."

This was the cynical, world-weary bit which had always found great success in my past. Today it fell flat on its face. The nice clean little thing with the pretty legs looked at me as if to say 'You really shouldn't drink so much, Mr. Thaxton.'

"You'll find Mr.Franks' office just around the corner, sir," she said in a voice you could starch a stuffed shirt in.

I gave up. I nodded and turned away. Then I looked back and said, "Hey. How old are you?"

"Eighteen." Still starchy about it.

"That's what I thought."

I went around the corner and entered the building with the word Private on the door.

Billie was coming down the stairs and she stopped and smiled and said, "Thax."

And suddenly I was seventeen again and standing fifteen years back in an Ohio stream up to my ankles and a very pretty young girl was standing on a log above me and looking down at me in a way that can only happen the first time, and nothing in this entire goddam atomic bomb-haunted world was relevant. Only that girl and myself and our picnic by a lonely Ohio stream.

I went up the steps and took Billie's hand.

"Billie—you just reminded me of the first time I fell in love. I was seventeen and she was sixteen, and it was the year I ran off to join a circus."

Billie's smile deepened. She was looking into my eyes.

"Thax, you're an incurable romantic daydreamer."

"Well—"

"No," she said. "Don't say it doesn't matter. It does matter, darling. It does."

Then she kissed me.

I just stood there. There's no other way to describe it. I just stood there. Billie squeezed my hand.

"Wait for me behind the nautch show tonight." She went around me and started down the steps. Then I woke up.

"Hey. What's with you and Franks?"

She looked up at me and her face, for all its inherent sensualness plus beauty-parlor perfection, seemed bright and innocent. Nice and clean—to coin my own phrase.

"I just gave Franks my two weeks notice," she said. "I'm quitting. Tell you tonight."

Her spikeheels clit-clattered down the rest of the steps. The door marked Private swung closed in her faint perfumed wake. I stared at it.

Quitting? No more Billie? Just two weeks? I was no longer the boy standing in the Ohio stream. I felt like an old overworked anachronism again. I went upstairs and knocked on the landing door. Franks' voice told me to come in.

The business manager's office was done in the same motif as May's suite. Swedish modern. It wasn't bloated with a lot of satin cushions though.

The bluff-faced Mr.Franks was just closing his safe and he stood up in his two-hundred dollar suit and came around his driftwood-Rez desk to offer me his hand. We shook and he asked me how Neverland was treating me, and I said "Fine," and asked how it was treating him, and he chuckled and said "Fine, just fine," and I reminded him that he wanted to see me.

He said "Yes," in a somewhat distracted manner and went back to his desk and picked up the phone and asked the exchange for Mrs. Cochrane's suite in the Queen Anne Cottage. He smiled at me while he waited for a connection and said:

"Sit down, Thax, sit down."

I sat down in a chair that felt like it had been growing on one of our hardwood ridges when Columbus missed America.

"May?" Franks said into the phone. "Thaxton's here now. Can you come over?"

He winked at me while he listened to her reply, to show me that it was really nothing serious—just the usual female nonsense.

I don't believe his wink any more than I believed his Swedish modern office. He was a natural-born yes-man who tried to cover it up with a hearty show of efficiency.

"Well," he said as he parked the phone back in its cradle.

That didn't mean much to me, so I said so.

"Well what?"

He raised his eyes inquiringly. "Pardon me?"

"You said well," I told him. "That usually means well something or other. I'm waiting for the something. The other you can keep."

His bluff fuse broke into a Babbitt smile and he sat down. We looked at each other across his massive driftwood-Rez desk.

"I simply thought it was time we had a little talk, Thaxton."

"We? Why invite my ex-wife into our little talk then?"

He fussed with his pens and pencils on his uninked desk blotter, arranging them just so.

"Well—" he said, "I thought it would be better if she were here. Because it more or less concerns her, you see?"

I said, "If you mean the murder of her husband—I suppose it does more or less concern her."

He frowned and made a geometrical pattern with his pens and pencils.

"You're a part of this show, Thaxton," he said gravely. "And you were once Mrs Cochrane's husband. I should think you would be willing to see us through this trying time."

"Um. As long as this trying time doesn't pin a rose on me."

He looked at me quizzically.

"Ferris is now toying around with two ideas," I told him. "One—I helped May knock over Cochrane, for money. Two—I did the deed on my own, for revenge."

Franks broke up the geometric pattern with his desk set by placing a pen perpendicular to a pencil.

"Is that a fact," he said solemnly. "I didn't know that."

I grinned at him. "Don't let it give you ideas. I ain't about to become the patsy for this smear."

He gave me an owlish look. "I can assure you, Thaxton—"

The inner door opened without a preliminary knock. May stood framed in the doorway for a moment, very dramatic looking in a silver skintight outfit. Like a redheaded shark, if you can imagine such a predatory creature.

"All right, May," I said. "Close the door and finish your entrance. You're on stage now."

She didn't get mad, which was out of character for her. She closed the door and approached me with a little girlish look of appeal.

"Darling," she said. "I need your help."

It was time to duck. I could hear the beautiful diamond-back shaking its rattles. I took another try at making her mad.

"What is it? Another corpse you want moved?"

"Darling," May said, "that's really very funny. That's the one thing I always liked about you—your wonderful sense of humor."

"Sit down, will you, May?" I said. "You make me feel like a rabbit in a cornfield with a hawk hovering over head."

She was too nervous to sit down. She started to pace Franks' office. We both watched her. It was a beautiful thing to see. She had the body for it and the body had the rhythm. But I had seen it all before. I let Franks watch by himself. I took out a cigarette and rolled it between my fingers. Franks remembered his social manners and struck his desk lighter for me.

"Darling," May said, "you've heard what they're trying to do to me around here." Her inflection said it wasn't a question.

"You mean murderwise?"

She came to roost by the arm of my chair and said "Um." She took the cigarette out of my hand the same way she always used to do and started to take a drag. Then she hesitated and glanced at it and at me, as if wondering if I had something I should see a doctor about. I took my smoke back.

"Everybody thinks I murdered Rob," she said. "It's all over the lot. Every last mother's bastard out there—" she made a broad arm gesture encompassing Neverland—"who takes my money is saying it!"

"Now, May," Franks said soothingly. "Not everyone."

"Be quiet, Lloyd," May snapped. She looked at me. "Well, you can't deny it, can you, Thax?"

"Uh-uh. But you can't blame 'em either, May. You're a natural for it. Look at the motive. Money money money."

She started pacing again, saying, "But dammit, I didn't do it! Why should I? Rob gave me everything."

"Uh-huh, but maybe you wanted everything except a sixty-year-old Irish husband. Maybe you wanted to marry some husky young buck who didn't have a dime and Cochrane said no divorce. Hell, I don't know."

May came back to my chair with little red glints in her eyes.

"So that's what they're saying about me now, hm? The dirty—"

"May," Franks said. "Now, May."

She whiried on him. "Will you for godsake shut up, Lloyd! Will you just do that kind little thing for me, sweetie? I'm trying to talk to Thax."

Frank's flaming expression seemed to say it wasn't fair of May to talk to him that way in front of an outsider. After all he was her business manager, wasn't he? He was just trying to be helpful and now May went and threw that kind of crap in his face.

"All I'm trying to say, May, is that it won't help us progress by losing our temper. We must remain rational and—"

"Rational!" May cried. "My God, look what they're doing to me! Can't you understand? I'm being framed for murder! *My* knife, *my* earring, *my* husband. My God, I'm as good as convicted!"

I stood up and mashed out my cigarette on a desk tray.

"Well," I said, "this has been pleasant, but I'm supposed to be out on the lot earning the salary you good people pay me."

May dropped her anger and switched back to feminine appeal.

"Darling—I really do need your help."

"Mine?"

"Um. If I ever meant anything at all to you, sweetness, I only want you to do one little thing for me."

I could have told her what she had meant to me but I decided I'd better not. I looked at her askance.

"What is the one little thing?"

I want you to help me by not telling the law all about our private life. I mean back when we were married. I'm in deep enough, darling, without having all the gory details of the past thrown at me too."

"Ferris already knows we were once married, May."

She shook her head impatiently. "I don't mean that. I mean, for example, that little incident in Decatur."

That little incident in Decatur had damn near cost me my life. That was the night I caught Bill Duff and May making like Ferris' crossed fingers in Duff's trailer. The night Duff lost his eye-tooth. May and I had pitched a beauty when we got back to our own trailer, and then May had pitched a knife at me and thank God I had decided to sit down on the bed just as she did or I would have had a new hole where I didn't need one.

It was pretty plain that a story like that wouldn't do her present situation much good. I grinned at her.

"You mean you want me to withhold evidence?"

"No, no," Franks said hurriedly. "What you mistakenly call evidence isn't germaine to Mr. Cochrane's death. It isn't relevant in any sense, except perhaps—"

"Except that it will give the DA a dandy chance to establish May's behavior pattern of throwing knives at her husbands," I said.

Franks looked slightly annoyed. "All Mrs. Cochrane is asking of you, Thaxton, is not to volunteer an old story like that if you don't have to. You see?"

"Uh-huh. Just a slight omission on my part."

"Exactly. And—" he took time out to clear his throat—Mrs.Cochrane would of course be very appreciative. I—uh, undertand you arrived here somewhat strapped for money?"

I cocked my head at him.

"You're offering me a shot at blackmail, Mr. Franks?"

"No," he said. "No no no. Please do not use that term,

Thaxton. I had in mind a bonus. After all, you do work for Mrs. Cochrane, and—"

"Oh for godsake, Lloyd." May looked disgusted. "Thax wasn't born yesterday. He called it by its right name the first time." She looked at me. "Will you take it and keep your mouth shut?"

I was almost at the point of asking how much It was, exactly. But I backed off like an honorable little man.

"This may come as a jolt to you, sweetie," I said to her. "But the only money I'm going to take from you is what I earn on the lot. But don't sweat it. I won't tell Ferris you once tried to use me as a bull's-eye." I winked at Franks. "See you two very nice people later."

May followed me to the door. When I got it open she leaned her lithe body against the edge and placed a silver-tipped hand over one of mine. She looked up at me with her best, practiced, feline, look.

"Like Lloyd said, darling, I am very appreciative." Her voice was pure cat's purr.

I glanced at her claws and drew my hand out and gave her a pat on the behind.

"Better save it for the jury, sweetness," I said. "You just might need it."

I went down the stairs with May's parting comment in my ear.

"Bastard."

Chapter Nine

A fog-mist rolled in from the sea that night. It was damp but not cold. It felt good on your skin, tingly and clean. It looked nice on the young girls' hair and on their outthrust sweaters. It put a spectacular halo around the high arc lights and made them a bluewhite. It was ghostly. It seemed to make the voices of the children more shrill. People moved through it like stalking specters desperately trying to seek entertainment, excitement, escape.

It was a good night for it. A good night, in fact, for a couple of ideas I had in mind.

The Viking horn went *hooo* like a dismal foghorn and I

gave away my last three orchids to three sad spinster looking females who had librarian or schoolteacher stamped on their tragically plain faces. They were very embarrassed and delighted and childlike about it. Then I felt sad.

I wondered why everybody couldn't be beautiful. If everybody was beautiful, then we would all be so busy making love to one another we wouldn't have time to be frustrated. Then we wouldn't jack-roll or riot or declare war. Maybe we wouldn't even drink ourselves to death.

Nut, I told myself. I closed up my stand and went over to have a smoke with Gabby. He said, "Hop in and have a drink."

I climbed over the counter and helped him close up. A single, naked 200-watt bulb made the place look like an interrogation room. The little white rabbits at the far end appeared to be frozen in their tracks with terror.

At least there were no effigies of Mao or Castro to shoot at. It used to bore me to hell to have to shoot at Hitler and Mussolini and Hirohito all the time when I was a a kid and would go to a shooting gallery during the war.

Gabby drew a pint from under the counter and passed it to me. It was Scotch and it was good I passed it back and said, "Coincidence. I was just wondering if beautiful people ever drink themselves to death, and now you tempt me."

"Don't sweat it. You ain't beautiful."

"My mother thought so."

"Mothers are nuts. There ain't any beautiful people."

I think he had something there, as far as the outer flesh goes. Usually the people the world considers as beautiful are sin ugly inside. Like May. But I don't know; I've seen some nuns who looked beautiful and I have an idea they were the same inside. Maybe not. Maybe they were frustrated like any spinster.

"Jesus," I said.

"What?"

"People," I said. "Life. Crazy. All crazy."

"Bet your ass."

"Well," I said, "it doesn't really matter."

Gabby took a good one and wiped his mouth and looked at me.

"Got any ideas?" he asked.

"Um-hm. I'm gonna go look her up in a minute."

"I mean about Rob Cochrane."

"Why should I have ideas about that?"

"Because I understand The Man has started to switch his sights from Mrs. Big to you."

I looked at him. He passed the bottle but I didn't take one.

"Where'd you hear that?"

Gabby shrugged. "Word gets—"

"Yeah, yeah. It gets around. I know. But who gave it to you?"

"Duff. Said it was from the horse's mouth."

I didn't much like the idea that other people besides Ferris were starting to look at me askance, or that Bill Duff was going around saying so.

"I just might decide to send Bill to the dentist again," I said.

"Somebody did that a couple of months ago."

"Yeah? Who?"

"Mike Ransome. They were over at the gambling room and Duff was on the sauce and he started to tell the boys an off-color story about him and May Cochrane. Nobody wanted to hear it because they all liked Rob, but Duff wouldn't knock it off. So Ransome put a fist in his big mouth."

"Huh. Ransome doesn't look like he could whip a Girl Scout."

"You ain't seen him in action. He's fast. Duff has the muscle and meanness but he had no more chance of landing one on Mike than I have of crawling in bed with Sophia Loren."

I said huh again. Then I switched the subject.

"Where is the gambling den? I'd like to look in some night."

"In the basement of Dracula's Castle. But they won't let you within ten foot of a cardtable. Not with your educated mitts."

"I know it. I just like to watch."

A legerdemain artist can never play cards with his friends. Not if he wants to go on having friends. Even if he plays square, the doubt is always there. Did he stack the deck? Did he deal from the bottom? Is he using sleight of hand? It makes everyone too damn uncomfortable.

"Well," I said, "thanks for the Scotch. I gotta get."

"Thax." Gabby stopped me before I could get out the side door. "You ain't kidding me, you know."

I looked back at him.

"What do you mean, I ain't kidding you?"

"You've got something going in brainsville, and I don't mean just laying Billie. I used to work for Madame Esmerelda. She made with the madball. I read you like newspaper headline."

"Don't give me that crystal gazing crap," I told him. "We both know it's as phony as a queer bill."

"Uh-huh, but there's tricks to it. You either learn how to read people or you fold up your stand. All I'm saying is, if you get in too deep, gimme the highsign. Maybe I can help you out." He paused and when he spoke again I barely caught it.

"Maybe you'll even need a gun."

I started to say my God why would I need a gun, but I didn't. I nodded and said, "Thanks, Gabby. See you."

Maybe he was right. Maybe I would.

I went around to the rear of the nautch show. My friend Jerry was there. He was walking a quarter up and down the knuckles of his right hand and he was talking to one of the nautch girls—a peroxided, overbuilt piece with a mean eye.

It wasn't any of my business. The luckboy was old enough to look out for himself. He had probably played with fire before and wore the scars to prove it. He winked at me.

"Show Bev how a real pro works, Thax. Let's see you take her bra."

"Is she wearing one?"

"I vouch for it," he said with a lazy smile. "I just felt."

"You dirty bastard," the sexpot said. She smiled at both of us—a real earthy we-know-what-god-put-it-there-for-don't-we-boys smile. She was about as tasty as they come.

Moving up next to them, I leaned myself against the board-siding on my left arm. At the same time I took her left earring with my right hand. She gave a little shriek of delight when I showed it to her, and when I handed it back I straightened up and took Jerry's belt.

They both laughed when I said, "Don't be too surprised when you let down your pants tonight, Jerry. I just lifted your shorts."

But he fell for it—his own game. I saw him feel his thigh, automatically, to be certain they were still on him.

"Ain't he the nuts?" he said to the peroxide bitch.

"Yeah," she said in a breathy voice and her mascara-blued eyes burned deep voracious holes in me.

Then I realized Billie was standing in the doorway just behind me. She was catty mad.

"Should Jerry and I go share a bag of popcorn somewhere, sugar?" she asked Bev.

Jerry made a quick smooth pass which spun Bev around and linked their arms.

"Time to stroll, doll," he said to her. He shot a last look at me over his shoulder, raising his eyebrows.

I smiled at Billie. She said, "Stupid whore," and I said, "Take it easy. My mind is still virginal." Then she started to smile and she said, "You damn fool."

"Where'll we go?" I asked her.

"I don't care. What do you want to do?"

"W-e-ll—"

"Oh honestly, Thax. Now seriously. I want to talk to you first."

I saw great hope and promise in that magical word First. I could afford to be generous with my time. I said:

"All right, whatever you say. Just as long as we don't end up in some kind of montage, like those actors used to do in the movies of the 'Thirties and 'Forties."

"Montage? What's that mean?"

"Well—you remember how an everyday slicker like Tyrone Power, say, would meet a poor little rich girl like Loretta Young, and how in one night he would show her the real and the entire soul and spirit of America, which was always exemplified by Coney Island?

"First we would see a brief shot of Ty and Loretta on the ferris wheel, which would blend into a brief shot of Ty and Loretta on the merry-go-round, which blended into a shot of Ty and Loretta eating floss candy, and so on. That's a montage. The art of arranging in one composition pictorial scenes borrowed from different sources which blend into a whole to create a single image."

Billie was watching me with a fixed look.

"Thax—how did you ever end up in a sideshow?"

"Kismet."

"No, seriously. You have brains. More than that, you have a sort of intangible understanding about people and—well—things. You shouldn't be pushing little walnut shells around."

It was a sort of lefthanded compliment. It didn't really make me feel any too good. You come right down to it, it made me feel kind of ashamed. Anyhow, I didn't want to talk about me.

"Well. it doesn't really matter, does it? Come on, now. Let's find a pint somewhere and go have our—uh talk."

"We don't need a pint," she said. "You smell like a moonshine still as it is." She gave me a mocking coy look.

"You don't have to ply me with liquor, you know. I'm an agreeable girl."

That sounded promising too. I grinned and took her arm.

"Where'll we go?"

"Come on," she said. "I'll show you."

The last of the marks were filing out of the lot. Their happy, or semi-happy, voices sounded thin and lonely as they trudged off into the drifting mist. Everything was closing up. Lights were going out.

One of Jerry's luckboys came by us with a mute glance, as if we were strangers. What Billie and I did was our business. He had his own problems.

Billie led me across the smoky drawbridge to Dracula's Castle, and to a side door which was like so many other doors in Neverland. It said *Private.* She took my hand and we went up an inky corkscrew staircase. Around and around in blackness.

I didn't make any mention of the fact that I frequently suffered from a touch of claustrophobia. Because more frequently I suffered from a compulsion of lust.

I like bed. I like the female form. I damn well like the lust of female flesh—in bed, out of bed, anywhere. I was ready to run up those stupid breakneck steps blind.

Billie opened a door. It was so goddam dark I couldn't see if it said Private or not. We stepped into a little room and it was like stepping into a page of *Ivanhoe.*

The floor was flagstone. There was a large Gothiclike archer-cross window in the outer wall and there was a canopy bed with high bedboards in one corner. I looked at the bed in the misty night light.

"Mr.Cochrane planned to make some kind of vampire roost out of this room," Billie said in a subdued voice. "The public isn't allowed up here yet. There aren't any lights."

Lights I didn't need. But I wondered how many of Neverland's employees had used this room for assignations. I also wondered if Billie had ever used it before. Funny how perverse the human mind can be.

"A fool there was and he made his prayer—even as you and I," I muttered.

Billie's face was a pale blur in the misty dark and her body was very close to mine.

"What's that all about?" she asked.

"An association of ideas. It's a line from Kipling's poem The Vampire." I didn't tell her what the rest of the poem was about. A rag, a bone, a hank of hair . . .

Even as you and I, buster. We're all saps when it comes to a woman. I reached for her.

"Not yet, Thax. Talk first." She led me over to the canopy bed and we sat down in the dark. It squeaked.

"Talk about what, for godsake?"

Billie laid back on the bed and I looked at her in that weird smokey quarter light and the last thing I wanted to do right then was talk.

"Thax, how would you like to get away from all this?"

That sounded like a line too, from one of those unrealistic boy-meets-girl plays that flourished in the late 'Twenties. But I knew what she meant. The tinsel and phony glamour and the buck-grubbing and the unadmitted fear of the atomic age.

I leaned over her. "How?"

"Let's run," she said softly. "Let's run away and not stop till we find a place so remote, so divorced from worldly problems that we'll think we're in Wonderland."

"The Wonderland Ride has a steep price tag."

"I've got the price of admission, Thax. Enough for both of us."

"You? How?"

"Savings. I'm a thrifty girl, and I know how to invest. I'm not as young as I may look? I've been coining the dollars for years?"

"Still—it can't be so much that it would last us for more than a couple of years?"

"You'd be surprised," she said? "Besides, two smart people like you and I can always make out?" She started to sit up?

"Thax—we could go to the Mediterranean? I've always wanted to see the Mediterranean Sea?"

I pushed her down?

"Billie? Let's talk about it later? Billie—"

"Thax?" Her voice was a whisper, breathy, warm, wanton. "I've already told them.—oh, *honey,* wait—told them I was leaving in two weeks. Are you—*oooh God,* baby, don't—are you coming with me?"

"Yeah. Yeah. Anywhere," I muttered. "Anywhere."

Chapter Ten

I walked Billie out to the parking lot. There were still about forty-odd cars scattered around out there and one of them was a squad car. Ferris must have been burning the midnight oil again.

Billie's car was a white Sixtyone MG. Cute little toy. I opened the door for her and she got in showing a lot of leg, which is what a girl has to do when she gets in or out of an MG.

A uniformed cop got out of the squad car and started toward us, coming in that casual, overbearing walk they use whenever they are about to give you some trouble. He pulled an aluminum-backed notebook from his hip-pocket and gave me a onceover that said "You ain't much," and gave Billie one that said "How much, baby?" I knew he and I weren't going to get along.

"What's your names?" he wanted to know.

"Why? What's the beef?"

"I said what's your name, buster?"

"Buster Thaxton," I told him. "What's the beef?"

He lowered the notebook. He was about my big except that he outweighed me with the harness and boots and badge and gun and all that nonsense. We sized each other up like a couple of surly male dogs.

"Thax." Billie laid a warning hand on my arm. "We work for Cochrane Enterprises, officer," she said.

"I figured. I still want your names." He was looking at me.

"L. M. Thaxton and Billie Peeler. She's Billie," I said.

He wrote in the notebook. "Occupation?'"

"We both work in the sideshow. What's the beef?"

He wrote in the notebook. "Where do you live?"

"I live in town, officer," Billie told him. "At the Regency. Is something wrong?"

He wrote in the notebook. "You?" He meant me.

"Tarzan's Tree House." I knew he wouldn't like it.

He lowered the notebook.

"Check with Ferris, if that'll make you happy," I said. "And now maybe you'd better give me *your* name. I want to go see Ferris myself."

He didn't like me any better than he had a minute ago, but it gave him pause for consideration. I talked like a man who had an in with his boss. I didn't mind making him sweat. I hate those storm troopers who jump on you when you're minding your own business and start giving you a hard time and refuse to tell you what it is you're supposed to have done. It's unconstitutional.

"There's no beef," he said. "We're just supposed to keep tabs on anybody we see hanging around here at night after closing time. There's been a murder, you know."

"Honest to God?" I turned back to Billie. "I'll see you tomorrow."

She gave me a bright searching smile.

"Two weeks, Thax. Then the Mediterranean."

"Sure. Night-night."

In two weeks Ferris might have me sitting in poky with a murder charge on my back. Billie drove off across the lot in the topless MG, low and sleek and white in the fog. The storm trooper and I started back to Neverland. He was still feeling a little edgy.

"You really know Ferris?"

"Uh-huh," I said. "I'm his prime suspect."

I walked away from him. When I looked back from the main gate he was standing in the big empty smoky lot staring after me.

Right inside the entrance was a big glassed-in map of Neverland. It was done in a bird's eye view and it was very colorful and carefully detailed. It showed me something I hadn't realized before. One portion of the Swamp Ride backed up to the manmade lake. According to the map there was only a rib of land separating the large body of water from the southern loop of the Swamp Ride's figure eight pattern.

It planted a little seed of an idea in my brainsoil.

I scouted around till I ran down one of the night watchmen. He was earning his pay watching the late movie on TV in the security building, which was just a small affair built to look like a Hansel and Gretel cottage.

"Hi. I'm Thaxton. I work in the sideshow." I showed him my magical card and asked him if he had a spare flashlight he could loan me and gave him some kind of phony reason for needing it.

It was all one to him. He wasn't going anywhere if he could help it. He gave me his.

He was a lonely old cuss so I hung around for a couple of minutes and helped him watch his movie. It was Mae West's *1933 She Done Him Wrong* and Mae was doing a very young Gilbert Roland wrong in the scene we watched. It was in this picture that Mae was supposed to have delivered that immortal line: "Come up and see me sometime." Which sounded like a line I should use when inviting people up to my tree house.

I thanked the old guy and got out of there.

I passed a couple of sweep-up men and another watchman but nobody I knew. Neverland seemed lonely and haunted, like a long lost Aztec city brooding in jungle mist. I heard a girl's throaty giggle somewhere nearby in the dark as I walked through the central garden, and then some rustling around, and it reminded me of that moss-beard kindergarten joke about the Simple Simon who stuck his head in the bushes to ask the young couple rolling in the leaves "How far is the Old Log Inn?" and got a punch in the nose.

So I kept my nose out of their business and went on my way, thinking, kids will be kids.

The one big light burned bluewhite over the Swamp Ride's deserted dock. The little *African Queen* type boats were all snug in their berths for the night. Nobody was around. I climbed over the rail and went along the dock to the far shadowy end and jumped down to a weedy bank. Damn near turned my ankle on a stupid rock I didn't see in the dark.

But I didn't want to use the flash yet. Like the couple who were misbehaving in the garden, this was my business. I didn't want company.

The fog was creeping over the dark water and coiling around the black roots and the whole slimy place seemed to be writhing to life around me. Once I was in there—what with the fog and the dark and the unearthly silence—it was actually like being in an honest to God swamp. I don't mean the little five acre morass, but like I had wandered into the Everglades or Okefenokee.

Tell the truth, it gave me the willies, like something monstrous was out there in the night—that even to look at was a sin, something that had the grisly feel of those man-eating plants that grow in the jungles of Malaya.

Then I remembered those goddam pet gators and I nearly turned around and took off for my nice high tree home.

Now now, silly bastard, I reasoned with myself. They won't hurt anybody. Everybody says they won't. I switched on the flash and took a hasty look around. I'd just had another sick thought.

What if they kept real snakes in there?

They didn't. I was damn well certain they didn't; but you get into a place like that at night and you get something like snakes in your mind and you just can't shake 'em out.

A mossy trunk-stump shook itself out of the gray mist like a shaggy black dog coming out of the water, and the flash hit it squarely and knocked orange glints out of the wet moss. It seemed to me the damn thing had a twisted mouth and that the mouth was grinning at me. I went around it like it was a Frankenstein's monster in damp wood.

I kept going, sticking as close to the edge of the waterway as I could. I wanted to find that little setback where I'd fished Cochrane out of the shallows.

The setback reared itself out of the swampy shadows as if startled at the approach of light. I played the flash over the water and the bank but there really wasn't anything there I wanted to see. It was that finger of high-ground behind the setback that interested me. I started walking over it.

There were a lot of tropical ferns and flowers and saw palmettos, and in about ten-twelve seconds I came out on the opposite bank and found myself standing on the edge of the manmade lake. The distance between the lake and the waterway was about one hundred feet.

That made one thing quite clear—the manner in which the murderer had moved the body from the tearoom into the Swamp Ride without too much strain and without being observed.

He—if it was a he—hauled the body from the tearoom to the Admiral Benbow dock, put it into one of the rowboats, rowed it across the lake in the dark and landed about where I was now standing. Then he or she or they lugged the body over the rib of land and dumped it into the setback. Neat.

But could a woman do it? Lug a heavy dead weight like Cochrane that far? None of the females I'd ever known could. Certainly not May.

I retraced my path with the flash, looking for footprints or heel-grouts in the earth. I didn't find anything except some of my own prints. Some detective.

I stopped. That old sensation of eyes on the back of my neck had come to me again. I straightened up slowly. The silence was like one of those transparent jellies you see in delicatessen windows. It seemed to hold me like the jelly holds the cooked partridge or the pheasant it is poured over.

I spun around and the flash sliced through the tropical growth. It made a white splotch on Bill Duff's face. He was about twelve feet away and was half concealed in the palmettos.

"Peekaboo at you too, Bill," I said.

He put up a spread hand to block the light.

"Turn that damn thing off, will you? You want to blind me?"

"Let's take a look at your other hand first, Bill. I'd hate to find out in the dark you had one of May's knives in it."

"That's real funny," Bill said. "About as funny as what you told Ferris about me."

He showed me his other hand. Empty.

I cut the light. I said, "Don't be nasty, Bill. It just makes us even. You've been hustling around telling everyone but Dummy Dan the Deaf Piano Player that Ferris wants to tab me with the murder."

"And it ain't as crazy as you want to make it sound," Bill said.

"Says who?"

"Says Ferris. He hinted as much the last time he hauled me over the stones."

"Which was the time when you told him about why May divorced me."

He grunted in the dark. "Why not? Do I owe you anything besides a broken tooth?"

"What are you doing out here, Bill? Returning to the scene of the crime?"

"Yeah, just like you. No—I saw a light out here when I was passing the Swamp Ride dock. I got curious."

It was a good answer, but it was still a lie. He hadn't seen any light. Not from the dock. Not in that fog with two acres of jungle in between. He had either followed me in there or he had already been there when I showed up.

"My turn," he said. "You on a treasure hunt or what?"

"Clues. I've turned P.I. It's a hell of a lot of fun."

"Tell me, so I can chuckle too."

"I had an idea that maybe the law overlooked. Ferris was getting all sweaty because he couldn't figure how somebody—maybe you—got the stiff all the way in here without using one of those swamp boats and without being seen."

"And you've doped it all out for him."

"I think so. Correct me if I'm wrong. You put it in one of the rowboats and scampered it across the lake and carted it over this hunk of land to the Swamp Ride."

He was quiet for a moment. Then he said, "You really are cute, Thax. Now do tell us why I did all this?"

"I don't know, Bill. But I can make a good guess."

"I just can't wait to hear it. I really can't."

"Well, somewhere along the line May dumped you just like she dumped me. Then a couple of years ago when you're down and out you read in *Variety* or one of the trade papers that May has become Mrs. Cochrane Enterprises. So you hustle down here and get a job off her old man. But May won't give you a second tumble and you're POed. So you knife the old gent and hang a frame on the body with May's name on it. Something like that."

Duff made a noise—a sort of mucus snort.

"I don't want to unhinge you or anything like that, Thax, but that same little theory also fits you like a snug overcoat."

"Yeah, I know. Ferris has already outlined it for me."

I could sense Duff grinning in the dark.

"I figured he had, Thax old buddy boy. That's why you're so goddam energetically trying to bird-dog it on to me."

I grinned in the dark too.

"Well, it doesn't really matter, does it, Bill? As long as we're still the best of buddies?"

"That's right, Thax. As long as we stay even." He started to slouch off to the right, adding, "That's all I care about."

His left came out of the dark and went off in my face like a cherry bomb. I never saw it coming and I sure as hell wasn't set for it. I went right on over backwards and cradled my head in a palmetto.

When I stumbled to my feet Bill was gone.

First thing I did was test my eyeteeth. They still seemed fairly solid in my gum. Good old bastardly Bill. He had been saving up that punch for me for five years.

I don't really mind an occasional belt in the mouth. The thing that frosted me was he had caught me off guard at my own game. He'd distracted my attention by making like he was walking off. I'd been wide open for his left jab.

I found the flashlight and followed the lakeshore around to the Admiral Benbow Tearoom.

Neverland was three-fourths nightblinded now and I didn't see a soul. Across the inky lake the rakish *Hispaniola* was snuggled against the black mass of Treasure Island. The stern lights were blazing festively in the schooner and I could hear the faint throb of music coming across the water.

My lips and teeth ached like hell. When Bill was able to land one, he had a lot of heft behind it. I needed a drink. I didn't especially want to row over to the island but I didn't know where to find Gabby and his Scotch at that time of night. Anyhow, he'd probably killed it by now.

I climbed into one of the rowboats and shoved off.

The fog was dissipating and the moon was climbing the black back fence of the night like a great cat-goddess. Its image was in the water and it was cracked into a million pieces and tossed about carelessly by my oarblades, its light all loosened and rippling wild.

Ransome had another semi-longhair piece going on his hi-fi and it pulsed a moody sensation through the moony night. Duff's punch must have addled my brainbox more than I had realized because for an absurd moment I half expected Mike Ransome to come dashing out on the schooner's deck, waving, gesturing, posturing, to stand unnaturally tall in that eerie light, facing the curtain of the stars and moon like some actor, some tragedian of the universe, addressing a great diatribe to the night.

I was a little punchy.

When I started up the gangplank I remembered what Stevenson once wrote to a friend regarding the use of the *Hispaniola* in his immortal novel: "I was unable to handle a brig (which the *Hispaniola* should have been), but I thought I could make shift to sail her as a schooner without public shame."

Just shows you that the best of us have our limitations.

"Hey, Thax!" Mike cried. "C'mon in, man. My God, it's good to see you! You can help me pass the long night. I'm the king of the insomniacs, you know, now that Dashiell Hammett is dead."

I didn't doubt it, with his nerves and the way he slurped up black coffee. I noticed the pot was perking on the hot-plate again. I nodded toward it and quoted Israel Hands: "Don't you get sucking of that bilge, John. Let's have a go at the rum."

"A drink?" Mike looked at me brightly. "You want a drink?"

"Do you have anything aboard this scow, Mike? I could stand it. I just lost a decision to your old sparring partner." I tapped my mouth.

Mike looked at me with an expectant smile. "Who's that, Thax?"

"Bill Duff. He landed one in the dark when I wasn't looking. My own fault though. I should have known better."

"Duff!" He grinned delightedly. "No kidding? My God, Thax, you could take three like him."

"Not in the dark," I said. "How about that drink?"

Mike clapped his hands and looked around the cabin.

"Well, let's see. I'm a coffee man myself, but I did have something around here. Ah!" He went away energetically and started rummaging a locker under his bunk.

I sat down at the table. My goddam head was starting to hurt now.

"Ho-*ho!*" Mike waved a half empty quart of gin at me. "Knew I had something left over from the last shindig we threw out here." He fetched the jug over to the table and went away to find a clean glass.

"A pannikin to wet your pipe like," he said, misquoting Long John Silver.

As a rule I can't hack gin straight. But it was better than nothing, and right then nothing was what I didn't need. I picked up the jug and looked at it.

"Squareface," I said. "Remember London's South Seas stories?"

"Do I ever! And how about John Russell?"

"Where the Pavement Ends?" I said. *"The Lost God?"*

"That's it! Honest to God, Thax, for sheer mystery, suspense, exotic adventure—I don't think anything can beat *The Lost God*. In the short-story field, I mean."

"Um. You ever read Morgan Robertson's *The Grain Ship?"*

"With the diseased rats? Good Lord yes! Beautiful! Both of those tales have that *The Lady Or The Tiger* ending, you know?"

"Yeah. Just like a murder mystery in real life. After all, who really gave Lizzie Borden's parents forty whacks with an ax? It's been seventy-some years and we still don't know."

"Or what about the Pig Woman case?" Mike said. "That

was another one, wasn't it? Or was it called the Hall-Mills case? I can't remember."

Neither could I. All I could vaguely remember about it was that some preacher had been misbehaving with the young church organist. Something like that. I fed myself a shot of gin and it went down like a jackhammer. The trouble with gin is it tastes like cheap perfume. But I had another. It helped anesthetize my mouth.

"So what happened between you and Bill Duff?" Mike asked.

"It's an old beef. We used to work in carny years ago. Just a hangover grudge."

He grinned and got up and said, "Well, it's your business. Listen, I've got to run ashore. Late date."

I glanced at my wrist watch. It was after 2 AM.

"Barmaid, I take it," I said.

He was busy putting himself into a bright, severely-cut sports jacket that was a trifle fruity for my taste. He winked at me.

"I like 'em at this time of night. The longer they wait the hornier they are. Right?"

I don't like people to ask me to agree to a questionable decision just because they want to pretend they have the answer. I said *um* and let it go at that.

"Make yourself at home, mate," Mike told me. " Finish the gin and flop, if you want to."

I didn't want to. Not as long as someone else was living aboard the *Hispaniola*. But all I said was, "Thanks."

"Jesus, I hate to run off like this." He seemed quite sincere about it. "But she won't keep. You know what I mean?"

I was glad he had said She. I nodded.

"Go ahead, Mike. I know the rules."

He flashed another grin at me and made for the door.

"Next time, Thax, we'll have a real talk. That's a promise. There's so damn much literature I want to hash over with you. Thomas Mann, for instance." He pronounced it Thomas Mon.

"Would you mind awfully if we held it down to Kenneth Roberts and P.C. Wren?" I said. "I know my limitations."

Mike laughed and raised a hand, dramatically.

"Aux armes! Les Arbis!" he cried—which was a quote from Wren's *Beau Geste.* He slammed the door after himself with a laugh.

In a way I was kind of glad he was gone. He made me nervous. His youthful exuberance was a little too much for my weary thirty-two years.

That's a funny thing. I felt more or less like Mike Ransom did right up till two years ago. But the day I turned thirty they pulled the energy rug out from under me. No warning. One day bouncing along like a rubber ball—the next day *Blaugh!* Flat on my face.

"Well, well," I said. "Here's to the young and hard."

I hammered down another jolt of the pneumatic drill. Then I thought to hell with the glass and I took it straight from the bottle. And then I had to laugh. The young and hard! That was a good one. Dirty but good.

Could I, if I had it to do again tonight? I asked my self. With Billie? Hell yes! I wasn't that old.

"Here's to the thirty-two and hard!" I toasted the bulkhead.

"Here's to Thomas Mung!" That gave me another laugh. Thomas Mung! By damn, I had a million of them.

"Here's to Long John and why they called him Long!"

Ho-ho, Christ I was murder.

I finished off the gin and got up and started stumbling about the cabin.

"And to Billy Bones who pulled the boner of all!"

I threw open the door and staggered out on deck. The fog was completely gone and the moon waited in the rigging, fat and proud.

"——— the world!" I announced irrelevantly. "And the moon too. I smashed you in the water, you bastard moon. See how white your face is? You're a coward! You can't face the image of your final dish—dissolution in the water."

Then it all came to a roaring halt. I felt sick. Godawful sick. I wanted to go to bed.

I reeled down the gangplank and across the beach and bumbled into the boat. How I got those goddam oars shipped and managed to row myself across the lake will always remain a wonderful mystery.

The next thing I knew Jerry had me under the armpits

and he was saying, "Thax—you all right, Thax?"

That peroxided stripper Bev was with him, and when I again made my grand announcement about doing it to the world, she threw back her head to laugh and her mouth looked like a big red fire bucket and that made me sicker than ever.

"Me and the water dish-olutioned the moon," I told them. "The water is the moon's slave but the moon is ashamed. I'm sick."

I threw up right where I stood.

"Jesus God my nylons!" Bev cried.

"Okay, okay, so I'll buy you another pair," Jerry said "Now shut up, huh? We gotta find him a bed."

"Let him lay in it, the filthy bastard," Bev said.

"Tree house," I told them. "Live in tree house with Cheeta, away away up in the rockyby blue. No You Jane in the bed. Just an ape. Like sodomy."

"What's he talking about for crysake?" Bev wanted to know.

"About diddling an ape."

"Diddling an ape? Is he some kind of a nut or what?"

"Yeah, something like that. A dead drunk one. C'mon, Thax! Pull yourself together. You can't sleep in a tree."

I had decided to be a stubborn drunk. The tree house was my home and that's where I was going to sleep.

"Hell I can't. Always sleep there. Get out a my way. Going up by myself. Going *up!"*

"Jesus H. Mahogany Christ," Jerry said. "C'mon, Bev, get a grip on his other side. We'll have to take him up there."

"Why the initial?" I wondered.

"Well, he can fall out and break his goddam neck for all I care. I don't like mean drunks. Getting that crap on my nylons'"

"He's not mean, just bullheaded. C'mon now."

"Why's Jesus need the initial?" I wanted to know.

We had a circus trying to get me up those spiral steps. And wobbling across that suspension bridge was a million laughs too—my rubbery legs moving at cross-purposes, and Jerry trying to hold me up on one side and keep on his own feet, and Bev straining her girdle on my other side, and all of us stumbling and lurching and me still worrying about the H in Christ's name, and when I gave Bev a friendly little pat on the behind she yelped, "Oh my God! Now he wants to make me. Like we didn't have enough trouble!"

"Well," Jerry grunted, "you've done it in worse places."

They reeled me into Tarzan's hut and aimed me at the bed with a good push. I collapsed like a bag of nails. Everything was going around like a fiery Catherine wheel and my stomach wanted to send up a rocket. The last thing I heard was Bev's voice.

"Hey, this is a cute little layout. We'll have to borrow it from him some night, hon."

I don't know when it was I had the feeling that little mice were playing on my shoulder blades, but it was still dark. I knew that without opening my eyes.

I didn't like the mice on my back. I wanted them to go away. I squirmed and muttered *uh-uh* at them. But they wouldn't go away. They kept scrabbling at me. Then I realized they were talking to me.

"Thax. Hey, Thax. Wake up, will you? I gotta talk to you. Listen to me, can't you? I got trouble."

They weren't little mice. They were little hands. That didn't make me like them any better. I pushed my face deeper into the leopardskin pillow and said *uh-uh* again. I felt bad. I wanted to die. I didn't want to talk to anybody.

But I wish I had. Maybe I could have helped the little guy. Maybe he wouldn't have had to die that night.

Chapter Eleven

The scream belonged in Dracula's Castle. It definitely did not belong in Tarzan's tree house because it wasn't a fun scream. It was pure terror.

It seemed to go off right under me and it went down down down, like somebody had pulled a ripcord inside my bed. It stopped.

I sat up. My head didn't. It was in limbo. My equilibrium went *weeeeee* and I sagged into tilt.

"Sick," I said in a piteous voice. "Sick sick sick."

I opened my eyes and they swam around like a couple of punchy goldfish in little puddles of pain. It was still dark but some erratic blades of light were slicing through the bamboo struts of the tree house.

What idiot is doing that? I wondered. Go away, idiot. Sick.

I became cognizant of a mutter of voices rolling up under me like a restless wave and I got all panicky. What if my sick eyes were playing me a trick? Maybe it was really daylight and the marks were rushing up to the tree house to marvel at me drunk in bed in my own mess.

I stood up carefully. I didn't fall on my face. Good boy. Now—first the right foot, then the left. I walked toward the open door and it was like wading through a room made of gelatin. My eyes were all right though. It really was night.

A gang of people were milling around on the ground. Most of them were standing over something just to the left of the base of the other tree. I couldn't see what it was they were looking at. About five of them had flashlights and were chopping up the night with white light. One of the damn fools hit me in the eyes with a stab of it.

"Hey, somebody's up there!"

Big news. I started across the suspension bridge but it wasn't as easy as it looked. It and my wishy-washy equilibrium didn't get along too well. I got sick halfway across and you would have thought I'd dropped a hand grenade among them the way they yelled and scattered.

"Sorry," I mumbled.

I made it to the other tree and gave the trunk a loving hug. Somebody heavy and in a hurry was pounding up the steps. It was the storm trooper with the notebook and he'd caught some of the curdled booze on his fresh tan uniform shirt and he didn't seem to think it was such a hell of a big joke.

He threw his flash right on me and it was like being hit in the face with a baseball.

"The smart bastard again," he said. He put a grappling hook for a hand around my arm and gave me a jerk.

"All right, stupid, down them stairs!"

"Take it easy," I said. "I'm not myself."

"You never have been, smart bastard."

He gave me a shove and I slammed into the rail and reeled to the left and bumble-footed down three steps and each spine-jarring jolt did something unpleasant in my stomach. He came right after me, laying the crystalline glare of his flash in my eyes again. Stupidly, I tried to take a blind, off-balance swing at him.

He gave me a quick short one in the gut and I folded over like a newspaper. But the people below were safe this time—I didn't have anything left in me. The storm trooper gave me another sickening shove.

"I just want to get you alone for about five minutes, smart bastard," he said. He manhandled me on down the steps.

My wind was back by the time I reached the ground but I was still in sicky shape. Indistinguishable faces kept shifting by me in the flash-splintered dark. Everybody was talking but nothing they said made sense. And then Ferris was standing in front of me and he looked about as happy as Abe Lincoln did when they told him what had happened at Bull Run.

"Take that john's gun for a minute," I said to him. "I want to see him about something."

"Save the static for later," Ferris said. "What about that over there?"

"The sonofabitch gut-jabbed me!" I said. "If you don't—"

"Shut up!" Ferris yelled at me. "I said what about *that?*"

He was pointing toward the base of the tree. I turned and looked. A couple of people stepped out of the way and I saw a little dark shape lying crumpled on the ground.

It was a very still little shape and it had small, pointed features and its eyes were open and sparking with reflected light and they seemed to be staring at me.

He wasn't wearing his apesuit, but Cheeta was dead just the same.

I was sitting at the table in the bunkhouse and a nice cop was feeding me black coffee. Other cops and plainclothes dicks kept coming and going while Ferris was trying to take his brooding stroll, and after he'd collided with a couple of them he blew up and yelled why didn't they all get the hell outside for five minutes, huh?

When we were alone he came over to the table and showed me his temper scowl.

"You sober enough to talk now? You want to tell papa about it?"

"Sober now, yeah. The whole trouble is I was too screaming drunk to know anything about it at the time. And how I ever got that bombed on half a jug of gin I'll never know."

"We'll worry about it some time," he said. "Let's worry about this midget now."

"I didn't push him," I said.

"Did I say it was murder?" he said.

"You're working up to it," I said.

He walked away. He didn't look happy.

"Let's take first things first so we'll know where we stand. I can turn in one of two reports and there will be no kickback. Suicide or accident."

He looked at me. I said nothing.

"What don't you like about the first one?" he asked.

I gave it a little thought.

"Well—I don't know the statistics on what percentage of midgets commit suicide, but I'll bet a buck it's mighty low. I can't ever remember hearing or reading about a suicide midget. Could be they have something inherently against self-destruction inside them. Know what I mean? The way colored people have an instinctive fear of dogs, or the way you never see a drunk Jap."

"Granny talk," Ferris said. "Come on. Why didn't he kill himself?"

"Because he was afraid," I said. "I don't mean of life—catching VD or losing his money on the stock market. It was a physical fear for his life. I've seen guys like him in Korea. They're usually the ones who break and run. And a scared man who is running for his life doesn't stop to take it himself."

"And Terry Orme was scared?"

"Yeah. I had a long talk with him a couple of nights back. He didn't say it but he was scared wetless. Don't ask me what of. I don't know. Then early this morning he came into the tree house and tried to wake me. Said he had to talk to me. Said he had trouble. It doesn't add up to suicide within the same hour."

"Too bad you were such a drunken slob you couldn't help him." Ferris said it the way he meant it. Disgusted.

I said nothing. I took out a cigarette and rolled it between my fingers. He strolled over and thumbnailed a match for me.

"What don't you like about the second one?" he asked.

"That's the easy way out for you," I said. "Nobody would ever question it because it seems so logical. He was always climbing trees, and everybody knows that if you climb trees long enough the odds are you'll finally fall on your ass."

"So what's wrong with it?"

"One thing—the little bastard was good at it. He could climb like a monkey, and I've never heard of a monkey having an accident."

"Let's not go into the statistics again, huh?"

I knew what he was trying to do. Bait me. The way the inspector of police had played the student-murderer in *Crime and Punishment*. He was pretending to seek my assistance, hoping I'd reveal one card too many in my hand. I turned clam.

"All right, you tell me. Why didn't he fall—accidentally?"

Ferris switched tactics in midstream. Now he was the harassed dick in the middle of a bewildering case.

"Maybe he did. Goddammit to hell I don't known. If it hadn't been for Cochrane's murder I'd never give Orme's death a second thought. Accident. Period. But..."

"But Cochrane's murder looks like a frame for his wife and I used to be married to his wife and I have a five-year-old strike against my name and Terry Orme and I were roomies up in the tree house and I've admitted we were both up there alone just before he took the big leap. Right?"

He looked at me. "Food for thought, ain't it?"

I actually admired Ferris. That's the truth. Plenty of dicks would look at poor little Terry Orme's body and write it off as an accident. These same hotshots would glance at the evidence against May and haul her off on a Murder One rap, and sit back to collect their medals.

But Ferris wasn't satisfied with the easy way. There was something about the whole thing that had a red-herring smell to it and his nose didn't much like the scent.

"So how much thought have you given it?" I asked him.

"Quite a bit," he admitted. He took a short circular stroll and came back to me again.

"Funny how handy you are whenever a body turns up. Have you noticed that too?"

I smiled and shook my head at him.

"You're trying to put the cart before the horse, Ferris. I'm never found standing by my lone over the body. Some body else always spots bingo before I arrive. There must have been twenty ghouls gawking over Orme's body before I made my grand entrance. Who was it by the way who drew the lucky ticket this morning?"

"An old friend of yours. William H. Duff."

The initial haunted me but I couldn't think why just then.

"Bill? What was he doing around here in those wee hours?"

"Said he was looking for you. Wondering what you were up to. Said he'd found you out in the middle of the Swamp Ride a few hours earlier, snooping around with a flashlight."

Ferris' voice turned casual.

"Any special little thing you were looking for, Thaxton?"

"Good old Bill," I said. "We should make a team."

"I said—"

"I heard you. No, nothing special. Just working out an idea I had."

Ferris spread himself with sarcasm.

"Oh, well, don't tell *me* about it. I'm only struggling on a mere murder case. The more information that's withheld from me the better I like it. Makes my little chore more interesting. Creates more of a challenge."

I told him about my rowboat and lake theory.

He just grunted and nodded but I could see it appealed to him. I could also see that he felt like saying a dirty word because he hadn't thought of it himself. And I knew I was right when he went to the door and told one of his storm troopers to scout him up a map of the place.

"You were talking about how somebody else always finds the bodies before you do," he said to me. Funny thing—that Jimmy Bently, the freckle-faced kid who found Cochrane's body? He's not around any more."

"No? What happened to him?"

"Dunno. I wanted to check with him on some little point last night. So when I send a cop to go find him he comes back and says they say Bently up and quit yesterday. No notice, nothing. Just gone."

Ferris hadn't decided to lead me by the ear to the nearest jail, so I was still a free agent. I should have been working at my shell stand but nobody around there seemed to take much notice of me one way or another, so I had something I wanted to do on my own.

I went over to the payroll office and asked for Freckles' home address. They didn't want to give it to me at first, but after a bit of con I convinced them I was a friend of his and owed him a sawbuck and I wanted to be certain he got it before he took off for parts unknown.

The address they forked over didn't mean a thing to me and a nice young thing explained to me that it was back in the pine woods near some swamp or other. Not far from Neverland.

I went around to the rear of the nautch show and knocked on the door and a raven-haired, sloe-eyed piece in bra and panties and highheels opened the door and stood there patiently while I filled up my eyes and then she asked, "Finished?"

I said yes and thanked her and asked could I now see Billie for a minute?

"Billie! Man to see you. Better bring your boxing gloves."

Billie was wearing the same next to nothing outfit except that she had a kimono over it. I told her I wanted to borrow her MG for a couple of hours.

"Date?" She said it kidding, but I could see she really wanted to know.

"Uh-uh. I want to look up one of the Swamp Ride ops who quit yesterday. Just an idea I'm playing around with."

"You mean about the murders, Thax?"

"The law hasn't said it's plural yet, Billie. Terry might have had an accident, you know."

"Sure, I know. But the word is already around that it wasn't an accident. That he was pushed."

"Who's spreading the word? Bill Duff?" I was feeling mean and it must have showed. Billie gave me an odd look.

"Thax—what's wrong, honey? You act funny."

I shrugged. "Beats me. Though something's wrong all right, but I'm damned if I know what. At first it was pretty obvious that someone was out to make a patsy of May. But lately I've got the feeling that I'm being slowly pushed into a blind corner."

"Wait for me," Billie said "I'll put on some clothes. I'm going with you."

"What about your job?"

"What about it? I'm quitting, aren't I? To hell with 'em."

I had a smoke while I waited for her. One of the rummy sweep-up men shuffled up and bummed one off me and wondered where a man could find a drink at that hour, looking hopefully at me, and then slumped off dejectedly, and then Billie came out in an expensive blue suit and we left the lot.

Chapter Twelve

Billie knew where to go. I drove the MG. She sat deep in the red-leather bucketseat with her head back on the folded tonneau and watched the sky. The wind made persistent little snatches at her candy-floss hair. It was just like platinum in the bright lemon sun.

We followed the feminine curve of the shore for a few miles. The narrow strip of pale white beach was off on our left and it looked lonely and end-of-the-worldish with its continuous line of surf quietly foaming like milk. Now and then we would come to a stand of royal palms and we would see a straggly clutter of meager huts nestled among the smooth boles. Fishermen shanties. Maybe some artists.

"Poor folks," Billie said with complacent satisfaction. "Can't live in the nice plushy Mediterranean like us." She smiled and curved her body toward mine and took my right arm possessively.

I decided I could wait to see Freckles.

We pulled into a blue-shadowed palm grove and parked in front of a deserted shack. The shack was shingle-sided and the shingles were very old and weathered and bowed. A battered dishpan hung from a nail on one wall and the window panes were opaque with scum and two of them were missing and had been replaced with age-curling squares of cardboard. A tall mending rack adrape with old rotting nets and corks stood at the north corner of the shanty, and in the blaze of noon the scene looked like a prize-winning photograph from one of the camera magazines.

"Come on," Billie said. "Let's go swimming."

"No suits," I reminded her.

"Who cares? Nobody's around."

She started stepping out of her clothes. I got so rattled I nearly fouled my zipper. I hesitated a moment in my shorts to see if she meant to go in in her bra and panties, but she didn't. She shed them with a quick smooth practiced precision and tossed them into one of the bucket-seats.

I couldn't help glancing at her underwear. They were nylon and they were very white and clean and I was very glad. I'm funny that way.

Say you meet a beautiful woman. That urgent something that is physical and yet not wholly physical and so must always go nameless sparks between you. You are both modern and sophisticated with adulthood and so you skip over that magical transitory period that other less worldly people observe which lies between the meeting and the bed. She undresses before you and she is graceful and careful and intimate about it and your passion is what the mountain was to Mallory. It must be satisfied.

And then you notice that her bra-strap is soiled.

What happens to your love? To your passion? And why?

I've seen it happen before. To me. And I never knew why. But this time I didn't have to worry about it. I reached for Billie.

"No," she said. "The sea first. The sea on our bodies."

She went away at a run, like a sea-sprite, her tan lithe legs flickering back and forth, back and forth in the sun, her hair like a shining white helmet. I went after her. I felt a little silly that way—running without any shorts on—but it was certainly time I got in the water. Who the hell knew when some idiot might drive by? My goodness, George, look at that disgusting man on the beach who isn't wearing any clothes! Yes, dear, but look at what he *is* wearing.

I raced across the incurve of the beach, over the lacerating hotfoot sand and took a flat-out dive into the glassy-water. It was perfect. Not cold, not warm. It was invigorating and clean. I came up and looked around for Billie.

She was wading in the tropic bay. She waded until water came over her breasts and then she threw herself forward and began to swim, doing it easily with a flowing, rhythmic overhand stroke, her head half under, mouth half filled with water all the time.

She swam in the direction of the path where the sunlight lay white as scattered moonstones on the blue water. I started after her.

"Hey!" I called. "Where are you off to?"

Billie stopped swimming and looked around happily and her wet face was like a tear-blurred shine of something very beautiful and precious.

"It's glorious!" she called to me. "It's like the Mediterranean. It's like our whole future is going to be!"

Right at that moment there was only about fifteen minutes of our immediate future that intrigued me. I caught up to her and took her hand.

"C'mon, Billie. Let's go back to that deserted shack."

"No," she said. "It wouldn't be glorious there. Here, Thax. Right here."

She threw her wet arms around my neck and kissed me. If she didn't mind drowning, neither did I. Not at that exact moment.

That afternoon we drove into a remote little settlement which was a bend in a country road by land and the flowing of one swamp lake into another by water.

There was a turpentine still and a general store and a huddle of shanties which crouched back under the cabbage palms and the pawpaw trees. Old Negresses had brought baskets of fruit, vegetables, tortoise eggs and black beans to sell under the shade of a tupelo. They closed up market in the afternoon by simply packing off their merchandise on their heads. The owner of the general store didn't seem too happy with the arrangement.

"Damn nigras," he growled. "They'd undersell a give-away sample."

I said ain't that a shame and asked where the Bentlys lived.

He was a beak-faced man in a wrinkled shirt and he gave me a sour look.

"You sound like a Northern fella. I suppose you're one of those damn nigger-lovers."

"I've never tried it. How is it?"

He gave me a baleful look and said, "Bently's is over there."

What he meant was a place just across a gallberry flat. It was a farmhouse and it had a simple grace of line, low and rambling and one-storied, and it had gone gray and cracked for want of paint. There was a tin roof and it was mostly rust, and the porch barely left you enough room to pass in front of the broken-backed wicker chairs.

It was Freckles' brawny brother-in-law who came to the door and he was about as cooperative as a wounded grizzly.

"Naw, you can't see Jimmy. He don't want a see nobody."

"I'm a friend of his," I said. "Just tell him it's Thaxton from Neverland. The guy who lives in the tree house."

"He don't want to see nobody from Neverland," the brawny one informed me. "Is that plain or do I got to show you?"

I had an idea he *could* show me. He looked like a mighty burly boy. I scratched my nose and wondered what I should say next. Then a girl from *Tobacco Road* came out on the porch with a bottle of beer in her hand and gave us all a flat look. She was actually something to see, bare dirty feet and all. Her voice was just about as you-all as they come.

"So mebbe he *is* a friend a Jimmy's, Flem. Why not let *him* say?"

Flem got hot about it.

"He said he didn't want to see nobody, LouElla. Hit don't mean a damn to me, but that's what he said, didn't he?"

"Well, mebbe this one is a friend." LouElla looked at Billie and upped her bottle of beer. Then she looked at me. "Y'all just saying you're Jimmy's friend, mister, or you another cop?"

"Ask him," I suggested.

LouElla had another swig. "What do you do at that Neverland—besides live in a tree?"

I grinned at her and said "Step up, gents, step up. One and all. The line forms on the right. Stagger up in wheelbarrows and roll away in limousines. The farmer wins and the gambler loses. Right here, right here, folks, to join the sightseeing party that starts immediately under the parental guidance of the Bay of Bengal. See the morals-shattering hoochykooch girls in their naughty naughty native dance. See the nautch girls brought at great expense from the sandswept deserts of the Sahara, each and every one with a movement like the Sultan's dromedary. See that intrepid swamp explorer James Q (for Cute) Bently. See him enter the jungle of howling beasts like Daniel come to judgment. See how the gators crawl on their bellies like snakes in the bottom of a DT's empty glass. See the savage denizens of the swamp cower before his manly gaze. The laughing hyena that eats once a week, drinks once a month, sleeps with his wife once a year. What the hell he's got to laugh about nobody knows."

Billie and LouElla were both laughing and even bully boy Flem was grinning like a fatboy at a birthday party.

"My God," Billie said. "How long can you go on like that?"

I winked at her. "Billie Peeler, ladies and gents. The Twist Girl. She can shimmy, she can shake, she can make your oh-oh ache."

Flem was all chuckles now.

"Do some more, fella," he said. "Make another spiel."

"See the zebra, the wild ass—pardon me, lady—from the desert of Africa. Note the stripes so tightly placed on the animal from the tip of his nose to the tip of his toes that every time he winks he sneezes and breaks wind and the nasty little highschool girls amuse themselves by throwing sand in the animal's eyes. Okay?" I asked Flem. "Do I get the job?"

"You sholy do, mister! Ay-gawd, ain't he a kick, LouElla?"

LouElla admitted I was a kick.

"How about a beer for y'all?" she offered.

"We would sholy love it, Miss Scarlet honey," I said with

a Civil War bow. "We would be forevermore obliged to y'all."

That got them all laughing again, and when my friend Freckles suddenly appeared in the doorway with a wondering look I went on with it to get him in the mood too.

"Wha' gawd bless ma boots, if yander ain't Massa Jim hisself, jes' back from stompin' those no-count damn Yankees in the wo'! Jim, boy! Light down these here steps and throw a kiss on yo Aunt Billie. But mind whar y'all throw it, boy."

The two girls and Flem went off in the ha-ha's again and Freckles looked at them with a bewildered smile. I was watching him and I didn't much like what I saw. He had the same scared look Terry Orme had worn.

"Thax," Billie said. "Stop it now. You're such a damn fool!"

That was the truth. I cut it out and accepted a cold bottle of beer from LouElla. Billie received hers with a dubious look.

"My poor diet," she said. "Well, here goes one-hundred and fifty calories."

Freckles said he didn't want one and he and I and Billie sat down on the porch. LouElla told Flem to come away and mind his own business. Flem didn't want to. Flem said, "I want a hear him do it again." LouElla had to stamp her foot and squawk at him. Then we were left alone. I looked at Freckles.

"How come you up and quit, Jim?"

"Well gosh, Mr. Thaxton. I just felt like it is all."

"Come on. Something's bugging you. It's as plain as those Van Johnson freckles on your map."

He tucked in his mouth, looking defiantly ashamed.

"All right. You want the truth—I was scared."

"Of what?"

"That's the whole trouble. I don't know exactly. I guess finding Mr. Cochrane like I did really upset me. And those darn cops on me all the time with questions. I mean like every time I turned around, it seemed like. That Lieutenant Ferris always sending for me, and—well—yesterday."

"What yesterday?"

"That Cheeta midget—Terry Orme? He gave me the

highsign from back in the jungle when I was taking a load of customers through the Swamp Ride. So when I had a break I went back in there to see what he wanted."

"And?"

"Well, I don't *know*. That's the whole trouble. He was real vague and edgy about it, you know? Wouldn't really come out and say what he wanted. Kept beating around the bush, you know?"

"Well, what did he say—vague or otherwise?"

"'Well, he kept trying to find out if anybody had been around asking me questions about him, see?"

"About him? Orme?"

"Uh-huh. That's what he wanted to know."

"Did he mean the cops?"

"No. I asked him that and he said no, he meant anybody else. Somebody who worked at Neverland."

"But he didn't mention any name, huh? Or anything that would give you a hint who he meant?"

"Uh-uh. Nothing. And I tried to ask him who he meant exactly, but he kept hedging." The kid looked at me with a look of appeal in his orange peppered face.

"And he was scared, Mr. Thaxton. I don't know what of, but he was real scared. He nearly had the shakes." He gave a sort of hopeless shrug.

"I guess that's what finally bugged me into quitting," he said. "I don't know anything about that murder and I don't want to know. I just want to be left alone."

"You mean you got scared because you thought there might be somebody on the lot who figured you did know something about the murder? Something that wasn't safe for you to know?"

He nodded. "I guess so. Maybe it's silly, but that's how I started to feel about it. So I up and quit."

I took out a cigarette and rolled it in my fingers. Billie gave me a match. I didn't think to offer her a smoke.

"Your sister—or whoever LouElla is—asked me if I was another cop. Have the police been out here to see you?"

"Yeah, this morning. A squad car showed up early. But I didn't want any more of that business. I skipped out the back and hid in the palmettos. Flem told'em I'd gone north. Which is just what I think I'll do," he added grimly.

I was damn sure he would, once he heard that Terry Orme was dead. I gave Billie a warning look. The kid would find out soon enough, and he was already too scared to eat his dinner. Why spook him ahead of time?

"Then you didn't find out what it was they wanted—the law?"

"No sir."

I thought about it for a while. Then I said, "That morning you found Cochrane. Is it the usual custom to take the boats around the whole Swamp Ride every morning before opening time?"

"No, that was just a freak thing. Usually all we have to do is see if they'll start up and then line 'em up in position for the customers. But that one boat didn't seem to have any poop that morning so I decided to give it a spin around the ride to see if I could work out the kinks."

"Do most of the employees know that? I mean that you usually just warm up the boats right there at the dock?"

"Well yeah, I guess so. I guess they do."

"Did anyone ever ask you about it? I mean before you found Cochrane?"

"No. Nobody ever asked me for the time of day—until *after* I found him. Now that's all I get from everybody. Questions!"

I gave him a benevolent smile.

"Well, that's what makes the world go round. Questions and answers. Thanks for answering mine. Let's go, Billie."

We took our time driving back to Neverland. I must have been pretty broody and abstract because Billie finally turned in her seat with a peeved look.

"What on earth's eating you, Thax? You act like an old bear."

I don't know, hon. It's just that I have an idea about this business but I can't seem to walk to it in a straight line. Something always gets in my way."

"Well, why don't you just leave it alone? It really isn't any of your business, you know."

"I think it is. For one thing too many people, including the law, sort of feel I might have had something to do with it. Well, that part's all right. I didn't, and I'm damned if I can see how any sonofabitch can prove otherwise. But there's something else."

"Well, what?"

"To begin with, there's Cochrane. I liked that old Irishman. I think he and I were about to be friends. Then somebody did him dirty. Then there's Terry Orme. I told the poor little guy I was his friend. Yeah, and the first time he needs me I'm too goddam drunk to help him."

"Well, it's a cinch you can't help him now. He's dead, isn't he?"

"Yeah, he's dead. But the bastard that did it to him isn't."

Chapter Thirteen

I gave Billie a phony excuse for not meeting her that night after closing time and she seemed to go for it all right. What I wanted to do was look up Jerry before he got off somewhere with Bev. I went over to Dracula's Castle and got directions from one of the sweep-up men and scouted up a back door with *Private* on it.

The stairs inside went down and I went with them to another private door. This one meant it. It was locked. The barker who spieled for the nautch show opened to my knock. He knew me and he grinned and said, "Oh-oh, we better get out the handcuffs before we let you in here."

"Just sightseeing, Phil," I told him.

Jerry was in there but he was just hanging around watching a poker game. He and his boys had no more chance of playing than I did. I wanted to see him but there wasn't any rush about it. I decided to stick around and watch a few hands myself.

Dracula's basement was used nightly for a gambling hall. The membership was strictly exclusive. Neverland employees only. They had about four tables going. Gabby was at one of them with Bill Duff and Mike Ransome and a college kid named Smitty. They were playing draw.

Mike saw me and waved. "Hey, Thax! Over here. I'll let you deal for me."

It gave everybody a chuckle except Bill Duff. He gave me a look like an oldtime western gunman ready for a showdown and started to get up. I shook my head at him.

"Another time, Bill," I said.

It suited him. He looked at Mike and said, "One."

Mike dealt the cards around. He was drinking black coffee and he hummed happily as he made with the cards. The others were working on highballs.

"Grab yourself a drink, Thax," Gabby said.

"Just a beer," I said. "Jerry gets tired carrying me home."

Jerry laughed and said, "Jerry gets tired buying his girl new nylons." It was a private joke and meant nothing to the others.

I went around behind Mike and drew up a chair.

"I sure hate to give a lamb a fleecing," Mike said, "but the lamb is *baa*-ing for it. Right, Bill?"

Duff scowled at him but said nothing. I got the impression Mike had been riding him.

Mike opened for a five, Gabby bumped five, and Mike stayed out. When the hand was finished Mike laid down his cards face up, showing two jacks for openers. He opened the next hand and dropped out again and when the hand was completed he faced his cards up, exposing two small pairs.

"You should have drawn to that, Mike," I said. "You might have gotten a full."

He just grinned.

He passed four hands in a row and then drew three ladies. He opened, drew but didn't better it, and got out. Duff won on two pair and Mike showed his openers. Gabby stared at him.

"Don't you like to win, Mike?" Gabby wondered. "You had Duff's doubles beat."

Mike chuckled. "Wasn't good enough for my money. I want a big one when I catch old Bill's purse."

He let another two-three hands go by, then he saw a ten dollar bet and raised it the same amount. Gabby and Smitty called and Duff raised a ten. Mike raised twenty. Gabby folded and Smitty saw. Duff tipped it another twenty. It seemed to be what Mike was waiting for.

"Ha!" He shoved in two twenties.

The limit seemed to be as high as an Irish whore on New Year's Eve.

Smitty backed out and Duff studied Mike with glacial eyes. Mike grinned at him. I started to hold my breath.

"No," Duff said and tossed in his cards. "I ain't getting suckered into that."

Mike spread his cards up. The best he had was a ten high. The expression on Duff's face was a thing to behold, and it didn't help his disposition much when Mike started to laugh.

I thought I knew what Mike was up to. There's three ways to play poker. Play your hand for just what it's worth. Play hunches. Play against the man who wants most to win. Mike was trying the third method.

The man who is desperate to win will usually overplay his hands. The need to win shuts out his luck. And if you can get him mad on top of that, he's dead.

Mike lost a few small hands and let a couple of fat ones go by. Duff was the steady winner and he was starting to perk up. He didn't think Mike would try another bluff. Duff opened with a casual five. Gabby stayed, Smitty doubled it and Mike raised Smitty. Duff called.

They drew and again Duff teased them along for a five. Gabby must have smelled a mouse and got out. Smitty hung in there, apprehensively, and Mike raised a ten. Duff smiled and pushed in two twenties. Smitty traded his hand for a drink.

Mike could hardly sit still in his chair. He turned to me with a happy grin and showed me his hand and I looked at it pokerfaced. Then he counted out four twenties and tossed them in.

Nobody said anything. Duff stared at Mike.

"Are you bluffing again, you bastard?" he asked.

Mike grinned, drumming his fingers on the table top.

"No," Duff said. "You wouldn't try that twice." He flipped in his hand.

Mike yelled and spread out his own, face up. Nobody could believe it except me and I'd already seen it. A pair of trays. A very feeble pair of trays.

"Aw for crysake, what kind of poker is this?" Duff growled.

Mike laughed delightedly and scooped up the bills.

"How about a change of pace, Billy Boy?" he said to Duff.

"Let's try a calm game of stud, five card."

"We're playing draw." Duff's voice was about as sour as buttermilk.

"But it's dealer's choice, isn't it?" Mike said. "And it's my deal, I believe."

Duff shot me a look I could feel at the back of my head Mike caught it and grinned and said, "Don't sweat it, Billy boy. Thax isn't dealing—I am. You know I wouldn't give you a fast shuffle."

He made the rounds with the cards. He had the spade six showing. He didn't look at his hole card. Gabby opened on a black ace. Everybody stayed. Mike went around with the cards. He got the spade two. Duff had a pair of eights up.

"Ten," Duff said. They all went along with it.

Mike's next card was the spade three. Duff drew a jack. The pair eight was still high. He made it ten again. Mike still hadn't peeked at his hole card.

He got the spade five on the next trip around. Duff reached for a cigarette. He now had three eights and a little boy showing. He pretended not to notice Mike's possible.

"Time to separate the men from the boys," Duff said. He gave the pot a sixty dollar tilt. I knew him. He played a hand for just what it was worth. He either had another eight or another jack in the cellar. Gabby and Smitty went home in a hurry.

Mike gave me a wink. "I think we should give old Bill a run for his money, Thax."

I didn't say anything because I wasn't supposed to. The thing that bugged me was the sonofabitch still hadn't looked at his hole card. He's stacked it, I thought. He must have.

I think maybe the same thought crossed Duff's mind when Mike started counting out his stack of tens and twenties and said, "I believe we agreed on table-stakes, gentlemen?"

I looked at his up cards again. Two three five six of spades. Was the goddam spade four in the cellar or wasn't it?

"See the sixty, Billy baby," Mike said, "and bump a bill."

Duff wet his lips, studying Mike's cards.

A full, I thought. All Bill has is eights over jacks, or he wouldn't stall.

Duff decided to bull his way through. He threw in five twenties and followed that with two twenties and a ten and said, "Bump again." Mike chuckled and started to count his bills.

"Now," he said, "the game grows interesting." He paused and grinned back at me. "The plot thickens, eh Thax?"

Duff was about as taut as a fiddle string.

"C'mon, goddammit. What are you gonna do? See or fold?"

Mike looked at him in mock surprise.

"See or fold? That only separates the pansies from the men. I thought this was poker? Let's see here—"

He lifted one corner of his hole card with his thumb-nail. I couldn't see it. Then he went back to counting his bills, first wetting his slim thumb on his pink tongue, and then shuffling out one bill after another.

"I have ten-twenty-forty-sixty-eighty-ninety, one yard. And twenty-forty-sixty-seventy-eighty, two bills!" He grinned at Duff.

"I've got some odd fives here, Bill babe," he said. "But I think the bet's steep enough for you as is."

Duff evidently thought so too. You could damn near see him sweat blood. His eyes bored auger holes into Mike's four show cards. I knew what he was thinking. We were all thinking it. No man would be kooky enough to try a wild bluff three times in the same game.

"I haven't got that much," Duff said in a small, tense voice.

"How much have you got?"

"Well—" Duff thumbed through his bills hurriedly. "About a bill—somewhere around there."

"Shove it in, old dear," Mike said.

"What about the rest of it? Pull it down a bill. I can't meet two."

Mike picked up his coffee cup and leaned back in his chair.

"I'm not an unreasonable man, McDuff. Tomorrow's pay-day. I'll trust you for the odd yard."

Duff didn't like it at all, none of it. I couldn't blame him. He picked up his hole card and looked at it close to his vest.

Then he showed it to Jerry with a mute look and Jerry raised his brows in a Christ-only-knows expression. Duff looked at Gabby and Smitty. They were staring at him like a couple of expectant hanging judges.

Bill Duff was beat. He folded up is hand. "Take it," he said.

Mike tipped back his head and let out a laugh. It was a high trill of pure delight. Then he got up and picked up his winnings and stuffed them any old way in his pockets, like the Scarecrow of Oz, and handed me his hole card.

"Give it to Bill at Christmas, Thax," he said. "I've got a late date on."

He walked away and I looked at the card while all the other guys in that room looked at me. I could damn near feel Duff's eyes smoldering in my face.

"Well?" he demanded.

I didn't say anything. It was better than the punch in the mouth I figured I owed him to just quietly hand him the card. It was very red and it had two faces. It didn't go with a low spade straight flush at all.

I drew Jerry out into the hall. He was still all ga-ga over that last hand.

"Have you ever seen anything like it?" he wanted to know. "I tell you that Ransome is wild! That was the bluff of the century."

Maybe. But I'd known Bill Duff a long time. He was the kind of cheap flashboy who begged for a cleaning. Anyhow, I had something else on my mind.

"Listen, Jerry. How are you in the Jimmy Valentine scene? Can you bust a box, if you have to?"

He drew back from me as if appalled by the question.

"Mister Thaxton! Are you suggesting that I, Gerald Malone, would stoop to cracking a safe?"

"Yeah, yeah," I said impatiently. "But can you?"

"No," he admitted and he looked disgruntled about it. "I don't have the touch, dammit. But Eddy does, if it's a simple box. What I mean, he doesn't go in for the soup and detonator bit. What's the pitch?"

"There's nothing in it for him," I said. "I'm looking for information, not for loot. So I don't think what we take will be missed. Nobody should call copper because of it."

"That's good. Because Eddy isn't looking for law problems."

"What would he want for the job? I could spring with my paycheck that's due tomorrow."

"Aw for crysake, Thax, you're talking to Jerry. Eddy works for me."

I put my hand on his shoulder.

"Well, amigo, one thing's for sure. I'm at least going to get you some new nylons for your girl."

Chapter Fourteen

This Eddy reminded me of the mousy little beak-nosed character who used to play in all the gangster movies twenty-five years back. Nervous, stuttery, with the predatory look of a voracious moray eel.

"What-what kind of a box is it?" he wanted to know.

The three of us were standing in the inky shadows of the alleyway between the storehouse and the bunkhouse. Lloyd Franks' office was right above us. Eddy's busy little birdeyes batted here, there, anywhere except on the face of the person he was talking to. He made me jumpy.

"I don't know, for godsake," I said. "I'm no box man."

"Yeah, but is it a wall-a wall job or an upright, or-or a combo or what? Know what I mean? What-what is it?"

"It's not in a wall and it's a combination box," I told him.

"Well, all-all right, then." He rubbed the fingertips of his right hand against his pantsleg. "I-I just want to know, see? What kind-what kind it is, see?"

"C'mon," Jerry said. "Let's get going before one of the security guards comes staggering by."

Truth to tell, I had my sincere doubts about this Eddy. He was so goddam nervous and jittery. But I dropped all doubt as soon as he took on the first locked door with his little pick-tool. He had that thing open quicker than I could have turned the knob.

We went up the stairs with a fountainpen-sized flash to guide us. Eddy kept mumbling to himself and rubbing his fingertips on his pants, while Jerry complacently hummed an old song about that masturbating, fornicating sonofabitch Colombo.

The thing I liked about Jerry is that he never once asked me why I wanted to break into Franks' office and crack his safe. It gave me a good feeling. A man who will trust you on face value is a rare find in today's society.

The door to Franks' office gave Eddy about as much trouble as I would expect to find in opening a cracker box. We stepped into the large room and I flashed the light at the distant safe. Eddy approached the box on a right oblique, sizing it up as he went.

"Yeah," he muttered. "It'll-it'll take-take a couple a minutes. Know what I mean? Couple a minutes."

I nodded sagely in the dark. He was the real article as far as I was concerned. He could do no wrong. I held the light for him as he gave the dial the first practice spin.

"Turn it-turn it off, huh?" he whispered. "It distracts my concentration. Know what I mean? My concentration."

Jerry was sitting in Franks' chair nonchalantly going through Franks' desk, drawer by drawer, using the moon through the window behind him to see by. He was still humming about that no-good Colombo.

"The captain had a cabinboy, he loved him like a br-o-ther. And each night between the decks they climbed upon one an-o-ther."

Eddy had his left ear against the combination dial, listening to the tumblers. He sandpapered his fingertips a couple of times on the rug and tried again.

"Seven-seventeen right," he mumbled to himself, "four left."

He had it open. I hunkered down with the pocket flash and started through the papers. I was looking for an envelope and I turned it up in less than a minute. Jerry had left the desk and he and Eddy were both watching me expectantly.

I didn't say anything. I slipped the envelope in my pocket and stood up and nudged the safe door closed with my knee. Eddy knelt down and wiped the dial with a handkerchief.

"What brand of hooch do you like, Eddy?" I asked him. "I owe you a gallon of it."

His eyes blinked from right to left and back again.

"No-no thanks. I never-never touch it, see? Not a-not a drop. It makes-makes you nervous. Know what I mean? Makes you too nervous."

The next day was a sleighride. Nobody was murdered and I didn't stumble over any bodies and Ferris left me alone. I worked at my stand with my little shells and that went well too. No beefs.

I closed up when the Viking horn gave its asthmatic moan, shook my head when Gabby made a have-a-drink gesture, and strolled over to the stripshow. The last round of marks was just filing out the front and it was rather interesting to watch their faces and catch what they had to say.

One lanky built slack-faced loner came out wearing a glassy sly eyed look and I thought it would probably be just as well if he had a police call that night or else some silly little fourteen-year-old gadabout switchtail was liable to find herself being raped from one convenient end of the beach to the other.

But it was none of my business. I went around to the back and waited for Billie.

Bev came out first and said something to me which she seemed to think was humor but was really only plain dirty, but I managed to cough up a laugh for her because her boyfriend was a friend of mine. Then she went away and Billie came out.

"Hi, Thax. What have you been up to tonight?"

"I've been drilling a hole in the side of the building here, so I can peek at you nautch girls."

"Um. It sounds like you. Won't you ever grow up, Thax?"

"Well," I said, "I still have hopes."

Billie made a wry face.

"Well, at least you didn't say it doesn't really matter. Where do you want to go?"

I knew exactly where I wanted to go.

"Let's go back to Dracula's Chamber of the Horny Vampires."

"Thax! Honestly. Someone might hear you."

"Do I care? Haven't they already guessed I love you?"

Her chin came up firmly and she gave a one bob nod.

"Yes, there's a rumor to that effect," she said. "In fact, Mrs. Cochrane asked me today what was up between you and I."

"So what did you tell her, the nosy bitch?"

"Simply that whatever it was it was my business, not hers."

"Atta girl."

But I was puzzled. Why should May care about what Billie and I had going? It damn sure couldn't be jealousy. So . . .

We entered Dracula's Castle and went up the breakneck stairs to the room with the archer's cross. It was a small room but it seemed indefinite and larger in the dark, as if the walls were no longer there. I headed for the bed. "You're always in such an impetuous hurry, Thax." I could hear the smile in her voice.

"No, that's been my whole trouble," I said. "Only at moments like this."

That was the sad truth, too.

There was no mist that night and the stars were brightly framed in the crucifix like window. I got up after a while and went over to the window and looked down at Neverland.

The night was growing. Most of the lights were already out and the escape-searching marks had taken themselves somewhere to rest. A half moon mutilated Neverland—long stripes of palms, shadow-scars of paths, mottles of buildings. It was like watching a dark tellurian carnival quietly thronging through a ruined and dead city. Or it was like a sleeping animal, a tiger of deep blue and blue-white, an enormous leopard.

"De Saint-Exupéry says the stars are like lights at the issue of a dark pit," I told Billie. "A man climbs toward them, and then, once he reaches them, he can never come down again but stays up there forever chewing the stars."

"Who on earth is Exupéry?" Her voice seemed hollow and disembodied, speaking from the shadow pool of the bed.

"He's not on earth. He was a French aviator and writer.

They used to call him the Conrad of the air. The Krauts shot him down over the English Channel in 'Fortyfour. You remember Gable's old picture *Night Flight?* Exupéry wrote that."

"Please, lover," Billie said, and the smile was in her voice again, "I can barely remember Gable. I'm only a child, you know." Then she dropped the bantering tone and said:

"But I like what your Frenchman said about the stars. I understand him. We see the goal and we want it and we scratch and claw our way up to it. Once we get there we can't let go. We can't ever again go back to the bottom rung."

I left the window and went back to the bed and sat down and looked at her in the dark.

"I wouldn't know. I'm still on the bottom rung."

"You won't be for long, darling. In another ten days we'll walk out of here and all places like it, forever. Um—that's what I wanted to talk to you about, before you made me lose my train of thought. Should we marry, Thax?"

"I don't know, Billie. That's up to you, isn't it?"

"What do you mean up to me? Why isn't it up to both of us?"

"Because I don't have much say in it, do I? After all, it's your money we're using."

"Thax. Don't say that, Thax."

"It's the truth, isn't it? I'm just a tap-city spieler going along for the free ride."

"Thax. Stop it. I won't have you talking or feeling like a kept man. It sounds dirty and it—it isn't healthy."

"Well, it doesn't really matter, does it?"

"Thax, I wish to *God* you'd stop saying that. Because it does matter. Everything that touches you and me matters because you and I are all that matters."

"That sounds a little tangled but I suppose you're saying that all that really matters is that you get to the top of the ladder and you take me with you."

"That's right. That's it exactly."

"Well, that's what bothers me about it. You're taking me. I'm not going on my own steam. That's why I'm starting to feel like a kept man."

Billie put a hand on my bare leg.

"But there isn't any other way, Thax. Don't you see? You're smart, you have brains, you know things, but you won't help yourself. You just coast. You always have—because you go around telling yourself nothing really matters. That's why we have to do it my way. If we don't we'll never do it at all. Not together."

"You can't arrange things that easily in life," I said , "no matter how strong your will is. It just doesn't pan out."

"Why do you say that?"

"Because it's fatality. Like us right now. We're caught in a current of murder, and when you're caught in a current you can't help it. Will has very little to do with anything. There's something inside us that makes the will play tricks."

"Thax, will you please forget about those stupid murders? They don't concern us."

"Yes they do, Billie," I said. "I've already explained to you how they concern me. And if you and I are in love, then what concerns me has to concern you."

"Well, what do you intend to do about it? You're not a detective, you know." She sat up in the bed. She was getting peeved. "Find me a cigarette, please."

I found us both one and lit them the way Paul Henreid did in *Now Voyager.*

"No," I said, "I'm not a dick, but things are finally starting to make a little sense to me."

"What do you mean? You don't know who killed Rob Cochrane, do you?"

"Well, I'm not ready to jump up on a bally stand and shout 'I know who done it!' But I've got a theory working."

"Well, tell me."

"'Not yet. I want to kick it around some more first. Maybe in a couple of days I'll throw it in the water and see if it floats."

That was the whole trouble with my theory right then. I was sure it would make a splash, but without more evidence to give it buoyancy I was just as sure it would sink like a rock.

Chapter Fifteen

The next day was like the day before. No problems, smooth as oil. That was the day. The night was something else.

I was working my stand and getting a good Saturday night play and my mind was as innocently blank as a two-year-old's. Then an arrow-paced whistle went by me and I glanced over at Gabby. When he saw me look he gave a slight nod with his head and I looked around and saw a couple of bad news birds coming my way.

I swept up my walnut shells and said, "That's all for now, folks. The hawks are about."

The two hard characters waited till my marks drifted off—which was considerate of them, I thought—and then one of them stepped up and drew his wallet and flashed a badge at me.

"Mr. Thaxton? Lieutenant Ferris wants to see you."

"Only two of you this time?" I said. "The rest of the storm troop on holiday?"

The man with the badge put his wallet away and said, "Let's make a deal, Mr. Thaxton. You don't make with the tired funnies and we won't tell you to keep your big mouth shut."

They were somewhat on the new breed pattern but not quite. The one who had flashed the buzzer was of medium height, spare built—a thin-faced dark man giving the impression of a steel hardness not wholly physical. I classified him as a tough baby.

The other one was maybe twenty-three. He had fair wavy hair like a halo over a youthful, almost girlish face. There was something a little wrong with his baby blue eyes and with the tense way he grinned at me.

"Has another body been found?" I asked, smiling.

"Ask me no questions, Mr. Thaxton, and I'll tell you no lies," the thin-faced man said. "Shall we go?"

It wasn't really a question. I shrugged at Gabby and the three of us walked out of the sideshow.

I started to turn south once we reached the hub of the central garden, thinking we would go on over to the bunkhouse. But the thin-faced man took me by the elbow, lightly, and said, "No. We're going to headquarters."

Something was out of stride. I didn't know what and I didn't like what I didn't know. But I said nothing.

We went through the main gate. The parking lot was well lighted and I expected to see a squad car waiting in front but there was none. There were only two or three thousand cars parked out there.

We walked along the north drag until we came to aisle 10 and we turned down that and walked some more. Nobody said anything and every time I looked the pansy faced guy on my left was grinning the same tight, plastic grin.

I'm not simple—just slow. I started to lag my pace.

"Uh—maybe I better have another peek at your buzzer," I suggested to the thin-faced man.

He took me by the arm again.

"Let's not have any trouble, Mr. Thaxton," he said levelly.

"Naw," Pansy-face spoke for the first time. "He don't want no trouble, Chad. Do you, mouth?" He gave me an elbow nudge in the ribs.

I started to take in my breath. The thin-faced man, Chad, stopped short. He stopped me. We were standing by a dark new sedan. I can't tell one new American car from another but I could tell that this one wasn't a police car.

A third man was sitting behind the wheel. He looked out the window at me with bright little piggy eyes that were set in a face the color of uncooked dough. That's what the glaring bluewhite arc lights did for him.

"Okay?" he, the driver, said.

"Okay," Chad said.

Not by me it wasn't. I pivoted like a soldier doing an aboutface and planted my right in Pansy-face's bread basket, and at the same time Chad gave me a chop behind the neck with the edge of his hand and Pansy-face and I leaned together like a couple of drunks holding each other up, or like a pair of lovers trying it English style.

Then Pansy-face gutted me and I swung to the left with a windy grunt and doubled over, and his upcoming knee brushed past my shoulder and caught me on the side of the face and straightened me out quick, sending my head toward the stars, and just then I heard Chad say "Enough!"

and I felt the hard, positive business-end of a pistol barrel in the small of my back.

"Sonofabitch tagged me, Chad!" Pansy-face cried. "Ain't no bastard on gawd's earth goan lay hands on *me!*"

"I think I said it was enough," Chad said. "Is that right?" His voice was very flat, very impersonal, and when you heard it you knew you were dealing with a man of authority.

Pansy-face backed down grudgingly. I think he was on something. I didn't smell any booze so it was probably a needle.

"Get in the car, you —ing mouth!" He gave me a shove.

The dough-faced driver had reached back and swung open the rear door and I collided with the edge of it. Pansy-face got me under both armpits and gave me a heave from behind and if I hadn't ducked my head I would have lost the upper half of it as I was propelled into the backseat.

Pansy-face followed me in and slammed the door after himself.

"Okay," I said in a strained voice. "Okay, I've had enough."

"You gawddamn better believe it, boy," Pansy-face snarled. "Or I'll purely gouge your —ing eyes out!"

It was important to me that he believed he really had me cowed. I didn't want him reaching for his shoulder holster with the intention of subduing me further with his gun. If he reached, he would discover that the holster was empty.

I had palmed his Roscoe while we were hugging each other and had slipped it under my belt when I swung away and doubled up. It was a twentytwo with a snubbed barrel, the kind that is easy to pack and doesn't make much noise and is nice for close work. I let it rest where it was because there was no chance to unlimber it right then. The driver was holding another snubnosed revolver on me while Chad went around the back of the car and got in up front on the passenger side.

Chad pulled his own Roscoe and rested it on the top of his seat, aiming in my direction.

"Go," he said to the driver.

Dough-face turned the motor over and punched *R* and looked around and we backed out of our parking space. He braked and punched *DI* and swung the wheel and we started cruising down the aisle, all the chrome bumper guards and exaggerated tailfins and red parking lights winking and gleaming and turning to a smear as we picked up speed.

"Slow," Chad said to the driver, watching me. "Let's not attract attention to ourselves. We don't need a speeding citation tonight. Is that right?"

"I've been here before, Chad, remember?" the driver said. He watched the headlight-illuminated aisle ahead. "I know what I'm doing."

"Yes you do," Chad said. His eyes never left me.

Pansy-face was starting to get jittery. He needed more action.

"What say we have Bob stop somewheres first, Chad?" he said. "The mouth here purely needs some working on."

He gave me a short vicious one in the ribs.

"Don't you, mouth? You need some exercise, huh?"

He worried me. His kind of bent-brain needed to feel power. He liked to intimidate helpless people. I was afraid he would want to pull his bobbed target pistol, to wave it in my face and make me cringe.

"Cut it out" Chad said. Then he said to me, "No hard feelings about this, Mr. Thaxton. It's the way the cookie crumbles."

"Or the ball bounces," I said.

We were out on the highway now and I could just make out the gray strip of beach with its pile line of foam running along on the left side of us.

"How serious is it?" I asked him. "Do I just get a working over from the hophead here, or are you going whole hog?"

"Oh, you're gonna be *mine,* boy," Pansy-face murmured.

"I wouldn't worry about it, Mr. Thaxton," Chad said. "One way or another, you've got to face it."

"Sure," I agreed. "But you don't have any objection about telling me *why* I've got to face it, do you?"

"I wouldn't know, Mr. Thaxton, I really wouldn't. And I'll tell you something else. I really don't care to know."

I had figured that. He was a sharp big-city hood and he did nasty little jobs like this on consignment. He tidied up other peoples' garbage for them and he never asked questions. That's what kept him in business.

"But you know who hired you," I said.

"Um," he said. "I know that somebody pays me. Beyond that point I don't sweat it."

"You know the name of the person who paid you this time?"

"Could be."

A night-owl kid on a bike missed death by inches as we whoomed by him—his gawk-eyed blob of face appearing briefly in our lights and streaming by to be swallowed up in the winged blackness. Chad's eyes flicked to the left.

"Didn't you hear what I said, Bob?" he asked quietly.

"I gave the bastard a mile's clearance," the driver said defensively.

"I said slow. Is that right?"

The driver eased up on the accelerator.

"Look" I said to Chad. "I figure you're passing up a bet."

"I've been known to do it before."

"Yeah, but I mean one from the horse's mouth. There could be money in this. Fat money."

He didn't say anything for a moment. Then he said, "They always say the same thing. Different words, maybe, but it always comes to the same thing. I'm being played for a sucker. I could grab a bundle instead of settling for peanuts. I don't know my ass from a hole in the ground."

His teeth flashed at me in the dark. "Is that right?"

"I'd say so," I said.

"I thought you would. Because they all do. All right, I've got to kill time anyhow. Go ahead. Tell me how I'm throwing away a fortune this time."

"First you'd better tell me who hired you for this."

"Oh," he said. "I see. You're just guessing. Fumbling around for an answer."

"But suppose I get the right answer? There is such a thing as blackmail."

"I'm afraid you're not very smart, Mr. Thaxton," Chad said "Elimination and blackmail are two divergent businesses. If you try to mix them you end up bankrupt."

At least he had made one point clear. I was to be eliminated.

We turned off the main drag and went down a lightless

back road at a casual forty. It wasn't paved. I could hear the pebbles banging off the bottom of the frame and a lot of sand or dirt was hissing inside the fenders.

"What you say, Chad? We have some exercise with him first, huh?" Pansy-face made another eager appeal.

Chad didn't take his eyes from me. He said no.

Thinking back I realized that the only time he had removed his eyes from me was in that split second when the kid on the bike had flashed by the car windows. That was good. He *could* be distracted. And a split second was all I needed.

Chad watched me. He said, "We close?" to the driver.

"Uh-huh. Any place along here. Nearest farmhouse is five miles."

I glanced out the window. A continuous murky scar on the dark earth was running along our right side. A drainage ditch, I supposed. Some kind of coulee.

"This will do," Chad said, and the driver applied the brakes.

"I'm going to ask you to conduct yourself with a little dignity, Mr. Thaxton," Chad said. "I wouldn't want you to kick up a row and have to put a bullet in you."

I wet my lips. The car had stopped. The twin beams of light converged and showed us fifty yards of drab dirt road rolling flatly on into the mystery wall of night.

"I see," I said. "A little incident is going to be arranged, huh?"

"A hit and run accident," he said. "Too bad about this, Mr. Thaxton, but business is business."

"Yeah, I know. The crumbled cookie."

"I did mention I was sorry, didn't I?" He didn't sound like he had too much remorse.

Pansy-face made a little giggle and leaned on the door handle.

"Lemme square him away, huh Chad?"

The door had opened about an inch. I said, "Any of you know what became of the hophead's Roscoe?"

They did what I thought they would. Pansy-face slapped a hand to his left armpit and Chad's eyes leaped right after Pansy-face's gesture.

I had the twentytwo out and I pulled the trigger at Chad's

chest but it kicked and he caught the slug spang in the Adam's apple and it must have been a dumdum because what it did to his throat and all over the windshield behind him was not pretty to see in the sheet of flame that roared from the pistol.

I lunged all of me against Pansy-face and the door shot open and we went sprawling through it and hit the road together, me on top, and then I started rolling like a log as the driver's snubnose went WOW WOW WOW out the window after me.

I got behind the car and came up in a crouch and I had to do something fast because in a second Pansy-face would have Chad's gun and then he and the driver would come after me around either end. I took a running jump into the coulee and it was like leaping into a well at night, only it was dry and it wasn't as deep.

I was afraid it would be loose shale but it was dirt so I didn't make any noise as I started crawling along it, working parallel to the road and going in the same direction as the headlights. The driver was yelling at Pansy-face.

"Take the right side. I'll take the left. He must a jumped in one ditch or other."

"He's *mine*, gawddamn you, Bob! You hear me? Wait'll I get Chad's gun." And then, a second or so later, Pansy-face cried, "Aw gee-*sus*, Bob! You see what he done to Chad?"

I kept on crawling along the ditch till that blazing streak of opaque light overhead lost its power of penetration and started to dissolve in the darkness beyond. Then I snaked up to the edge of the parapet and looked back down the road.

The car's headlights glowered at me like jack-o-lantern eyes. Pansy-face's silhouette cut across them. He was holding Chad's pistol at hip-level. I eased myself out of the ditch and sat down in the road facing the car and tested my gunarm on my cocked right knee and gave it support with my other hand and took a sight and called, "Down here."

Pansy-face spun around with the front of the car at his back and gave me a beautiful fullfront silhouette. I squeezed off but it went high again and nabbed him in the neck and threw him back against the nose of the hood.

Then his knees buckled and he went down in the road like a dropped shirt.

I only caught a flicker impression of the driver piling back into the car and I snapped one at him but God knows where it went. The motor was still idling and all he had to do was flip off the emergency and punch a button and give it the gas.

But he forgot about Pansy-face.

"Jesus Christ, Bob, wa—!"

The car lurched forward and went *thump* over the meaty obstacle and a shriek like I never want to hear again ripped the fabric of the night.

The driver was already rattled and the good-god realization that he had just mashed Pansy-face must have unglued him completely. He floored it and that big rumbling crystal-eyed sedan came hurtling down the road at me, but it was already slated for crashville when I started jerking off shots at the windshield, and it swerved out of control and to the left and I took a frantic roll back into the ditch.

The tires howled and the brakes started to scream and all of it went into a great metallic crash and seemed to surround me in a shivering glass ball of sound. Then it popped and all I could hear was the quiet, tentative giving of ruptured metal parts and the *plippity-plip* of draining liquid puddling. The headlights were burning steadily at a crazy tilt.

I climbed out of the ditch and went across the road and looked down the other side. The car had turned turtle on the slope. It was on its top and two of the tractionless wheels were still spinning. The driver was partly out the window and he was in a crumple on his head and shoulders. The black liquid running over his face looked like oil but of course it wasn't.

I went down the road and looked at Pansy-face. His legs were at an odd angle to his body and he was hemorrhaging from the mouth. I hoped he hadn't died right away.

I wiped off the pistol and pitched it in the field by the wreck. I didn't see any reason why I should get involved with the law—any more than I already was. I started hoofing back the way we had come.

Chapter Sixteen

It cost me an hour to reach the highway and another halfhour to find an all night coffee stand. I phoned for a taxi from there and it was 12:45 when I paid off the hack in front of Billie's apartment, the Regency.

Billie was getting ready for bed and she was in one of those skimpy nylon nighties that end where Eve wore the fig leaf. She looked at me as if I'd just dropped out of the moon.

"Why, Thax!"

I stepped into her room and closed the door and said, "I had a little trouble."

She gave me a half wondering, half critical look.

"You look like you've been rolling in it. What happened?"

I told her it was a car accident.

"Well, whose car? Was anybody hurt?"

"Nobody was hurt. Just three guys were killed. Okay I use your bathroom? I feel as grimy as a Union Pacific engineer."

I told her about it after I got out of the shower and put my shorts back on. "It was an anachronism. An honest to God old-fashioned ride. Like something out of the *Little Caesar* days."

"But *why*, Thax? Who would want to do such a crazy thing to you?"

"Someone who figures I'm getting too smart."

"You mean the same person who killed Rob Cochrane and Terry Orme?"

I shook my head and asked her if she had a drink around there. After-reaction was setting in and I suddenly needed a drink very badly. She had bourbon.

"No," I told her. "It wasn't the same person. The person who fixed Cochrane and Orme does his own dirty-work. This Edward G. Robinson-type ride is someone else's style."

Billie looked annoyed. "I don't understand. Just how many people at Neverland have homicidal tendencies?"

I grinned at her. "One too many. That's what had me

going in circles so long. I didn't figure it that way."

"Honestly, Thax. You're the most maddening person I know. Are you going to tell me what it's all about, or just leave me up in the air?"

"Up in the air is one place I'm not going to leave you. Not while there's a nice warm bed waiting ten feet away. Shut up now like a good little girl, huh? And come to daddy."

I didn't want to talk about murder. I had just been too damn close to my own. I had been lucky and now I was full of the joy of living and I had to do something vital and energetic to establish my love of life.

"Really, Thax," Billie said. "Sometimes I wonder about you." But she was smiling.

I took her by the hand and walked the ten feet.

We drove to Neverland around noon. We had decided I should find myself a room somewhere. There were no doors I could lock in Tarzan's hut and it was no longer a very safe place for me to sleep in.

"I've got a couple of clean shirts and whatnot tucked under Tarzan's bed," I told her. "I'll pick'em up after we close tonight and meet you at the main gate."

"Thax," Billie said, "be careful. Don't trust anyone."

"Stop worrying about it, will you?"

"I can't help worrying about it. We're so close to everything I've ever wanted. In another week we'll be starting out for a glorious new life."

I nodded, thinking about it, looking at Neverland.

"Like conquistadors in a fabled city, plundering the treasure vaults of their frozen jewels," I said.

"What's that supposed to mean?"

"Just something else de Saint-Exupéry said about aviators and the stars. It doesn't matter."

Billie looked at me doubtfully.

"Well, I'm afraid I don't see the connection," she said. "But just the same, don't do anything to spoil it."

"Don't worry," I said. "I'll take care of myself. See you tonight."

I was never more wrong in my life. I wasn't going to see her that night and someone else was going to take care of me. I had forgotten that a man's will has very little to say about the direction he is going when he is caught in a current.

It was a hot, almost sultry day with no help from the sea, and we had a good crowd. I worked my stand for a few hours but my mind wasn't on it. I kept waiting for something to happen and when nothing did I began to wonder if I'd been wrong.

The way I figured it a crack had to appear in the egg-shell soon so that the chick could show its beak. When it didn't, I started to get nervous.

I stayed at my stand till about four and then I went over to Gabby's gallery.

"Smoke break," I said.

He was agreeable. He said, "Want a snort?"

"No. But let's step around back a minute."

We went around to the little tented area and lit up. There was a small locked shack back there and I knew he kept his twentytwos and live ammo inside.

I said, "Look, Gabby. You mentioned something about if I ever needed a gun."

He gave me a sharp look and forgot to drag on his smoke. "Has it come to that, Thax?"

I shrugged. "I've got a funny feeling it might."

My funny feeling was a matter of nerves. I was getting spooky with suspense. Nothing was happening when I damn well knew that something *should* happen. Everything pointed to it.

The corners of Gabby's mouth dipped into points.

"Why don't you use your head, Thax, and cut and run?"

"I'm in too deep. I've got to go along with it."

"You mean you *want* to go along with it," Gabby said.

I thought about it. Maybe he was right, and maybe he had just put his finger on the cracked keystone of my character. I had been content to drift as a nonentity through a life I didn't understand or like, blaming my inadequacy on fate, when it was actually my own gutlessness that kept me a nothing, a Then person.

This train of thought was more of an emotion than an idea and the emotion had a personification. The picture I suddenly saw of myself made me lonely, empty, and it filled me with distaste.

"Well" I said defensively "it doesn't really matter, does it?

Because one way or another I'm going to see the end of it."

"Yeah," Gabby said, "and I think you're a goddam sap."

"You ain't alone in that thought. But can you help me or not?"

He made points with his mouth again.

"That's the thing. I *ain't* helping you any by giving you a gun."

"Look, Gabby. Let's not make with the pseudo-profound platitudes. Let's just call it backass help and let it go at that."

"Well, but you don't want to go wandering around with a twentytwo rifle over your shoulder like a goddam sentry, do you?"

No, I didn't want to do that. In fact I'd been thinking about kicking myself because I'd been so goddarn hasty in throwing away that pistol the night before.

"Look," I said. "A couple of days back you offered me the loan of a gun if I thought I needed one. You weren't thinking about a twentytwo then, were you?"

Gabby scowled at the ground. "No," he admitted. "I've got a Roscoe put away—but you're a damn fool if you try to use it."

"Gabby—let me sweat it, will you? How about it? Do I get the Roscoe?"

Gabby shrugged. "It's your neck."

He unlocked the shack door and went inside and made some noise and climbed out again with an automatic in his hand. He didn't look one bit happy about it when he passed over the weapon.

It was a fortyfive, a Colt. I thumbed the clip latch and extracted the magazine. It was loaded. I palmed it home and pulled the slide and made sure the safety was on. Then I shoved it under my belt and buttoned my jacket over it and nodded at Gabby.

"Maybe I won't have to use it," I said.

He looked at me and said, "I hope not. I hope you figure out another way."

"Maybe somebody will figure out another way for me," I said.

The funny thing was—somebody already had.

Nothing happened. Six o'clock ticked around and I knocked off and went over to the Queen Anne Cottage and had a New York cut and amused myself kidding with the cute waitress over my smoke and coffee.

I asked her what she thought of *Treasure Island* and she told me she had gone over there one night with one of the college boys who worked on the lot and had *she* ever had a time fighting him off, and I said no I meant the book, and she gave me a blank look and said huh? Then she said oh and went on to tell me that *Treasure Island* was just a kid's book.

"You're only half right," I said. "*Treasure Island* was written for those who won't let youth slip away. For those whose attitude toward life has not been ruined by life."

She gave me a look that was supposed to imply that I just might be some kind of nut.

"I can't imagine what you think you're talking about."

"Neither can I," I said. "Because my attitude doesn't fit in that picture. I've already been ruined for life by sexy young things like you."

Now we were on her ground. She laughed and called me naughty and went rump-twitching on about her business. I spent a few seconds meditating on her locomotion, as viewed from the rear, and then I thought about *Treasure Island* again.

The big clincher moment in the tale had been when Jim Hawkins and John Silver, George Merry, Tom Morgan and the lad known as Dick arrive at Flint's treasure cache and find that the map they have carefully followed is wrong. The treasure had been moved.

There never was such an overturn in this world, Stevenson had written about the pirates' shocked emotion.

I finished my coffee and went back to my stand and still nothing happened. Bill Duff had been giving me peculiar stares for about an hour, and finally around eight or so he strolled over and said hi.

"Bill," I replied. I showed him the little pea and covered it and made a right-over-left pass and he tapped the right shell with his finger. I didn't palm it because there was no profit in it. Anyhow, he had something on his mind and I didn't want to derail his train of thought.

"You want your orchid gift wrapped?" I asked him.

"Keep it for your bitch," he told me.

I was curious about what had brought him over to see me so I didn't get mad at that. Duff didn't look at me. He toyed with one of my walnut shells.

"I've been thinking, Thax, that you and I are a couple of saps."

"I'll go along with half of that," I said. "I've been thinking that one of us was."

He gave me the lovable old Duff dagger look.

"No, I'm serious. We've been at loggerheads when if we had any brains we'd be a team. You know what I mean?"

"Uh-huh, and it's a funny thing. I said the same thing to Ferris not so long ago."

"You did?"

"Uh-huh. A slapstick team. You slap a pie in my face and then I plaster your face."

"No, no, for godsake. I don't mean the cutthroat way we've always acted. I mean we should start putting our heads together. You know?"

"Like the two-headed calf in the illusion show."

He gave me an aggrieved but patient look and said, "Will you knock off the hilarity? I'm serious. And you *know* what I'm talking about. I figure together we could both do ourselves some good. Some real good."

"Well, Bill, everybody's opinion is worth something. Even a clock that's stopped is right twice a day. What is it that you want to share with me?"

"C'mon," he snapped. "You know as well as I do what the score is. There's a fortune in it."

"Um. I said that to a man last night and nearly got my head blown off." I started to rotate the walnut shells.

"The trouble with you, Bill, is you want to go fishing with my bait. You're seeing about a yard beyond Ferris' view—while I'm looking at the whole vista. No deal."

I raised my head and started a spiel.

"This way, ladies and gentlemen! The one cylinder ball-bearing ride is about to start again. Three little tepees with a little white medicine ball. Step aside, mister, let the little lady with the pretty face see the white rabbit." I looked at Duff.

He gave me an icepick look and walked away.

The funny thing is that for the first time in the seven

years I had known Duff, I felt sorry for him. A little. He, like most of us, had a hunger that could never be gratified in this life. But for a brief moment he had had a glimpse at the menu—just before I slammed the door in his face and hung out the Closed Indefinitely sign.

"The little lady's shriek of delight is a wail of woe in the gambler's ear," I said as I handed over a dime-a-dozen orchid to the girl with the pretty face.

The Viking horn moaned and the marks started their noisy, confused, semi-happy evacuation. There would probably be much misbehaving in the cars in the parking lot that night and you could risk a guess that there would be a few inevitable results in about nine months and maybe even a few venereal catastrophes a hell of a lot sooner.

But as far as I was concerned nothing had happened.

I went up to the treehouse to dig out my spare shirts and shorts and socks. The truth was, I felt a little sad about leaving Tarzan's hut. Maybe I was too much like those who wouldn't let youth slip by, like Peter Pan or Mike Ransome. Maybe I was doomed to bumble through life without ever realizing total maturity.

"Well," I thought, "it doesn't matter, does it? So I like to live in a tree house. What's so goddam wrong in that?"

I pulled out the Coke bottle carton which I kept my spare shirts and underwear in and I stared at it in the brilliant light of Terry Orme's Coleman lantern. And with an odd sense of unreality I felt the world turn back twenty-some years—back to the first time I read *Treasure Island* and came to the part where Blind Pew put the piece of paper in Billy Bones' rum-palsied hand.

A little round piece of paper was pinned to my top shirt. It was black on one side and white on the other, words had been printed on the white side.

One o'clock.

Chapter Seventeen

But *what is the black spot, captain?* Jim Hawkins had asked. *That's a summons, mate,* Billy Bones had answered.

And that's what this black spot was—a summons for me. Because the person who had planted it on my shirt knew me. Knew my immature sense of the dramatic. Knew I wouldn't call cop.

And he was right. Like John Silver I had to bullhead a bad deal out to the bitter end. I touched the plastic butted reassurance of the fortyfive under my jacket and grinned.

"Nobody," I thought, "ever got the best of Silver. Not even Ben Gunn."

I left the tree house and went down to the Admiral Benbow. The *Hispaniola* was moored for the night against Treasure Island. The stern windows were open and a blocky shaft of light was jabbing through them and making an orange puddle on the shallow water under the schooner's counter. Soft music throbbed over the dark man made lake.

I got in a boat and rowed to the island.

The cabin door flew open and Mike Ransome stood in the flood of light grinning at me.

"Thax! I've been expecting you."

I held out the black spot to him and made another stab at quoting Silver.

"Look here. This ain't lucky. You've gone and cut a Bible. What fool has cut a Bible?"

Mike took the black spot and chuckled.

"It was Dick," he said, quoting loosely, "and he can get to prayers. He's seen his slice of luck, has Dick, and you may lay to that."

"Amen," I said.

Mike made a gesture inviting me in. Then he took a quick look behind me before he closed the door.

"Come alone, Thax? I rather thought you would."

"Sure. Just like you said the first time we met, Master Gunn—'Him that comes is to have a white thing in his hand and he's to come alone.' Remember?"

I took a casual turn around the cabin. The hi-fi was still purring soft mood music. There was a triangular wardrobe in the angle between the forward bulkhead and the starboard wall. It was faced with two louver doors and I got the impression that the righthand door shifted slightly as I walked by. I went to the stern and parked my prat on one of the open window frames, folded my arms and smiled at Mike.

He wagged the black spot at me. "It really was cut from a Bible, Thax. I always keep one around for laughs. I thought it was the perfect touch. You agree?"

"That's right. I couldn't resist it. You must be uncanny, Mike. You seem to know me like a book."

Mike looked delighted. "Care for a drink?"

"Uh—no thanks. That last one I had out here was murder. I mean that in the literal sense."

Mike chuckled and went over to the hi-fi and killed the music.

"You put something in that gin, didn't you?" I said.

He was enjoying himself immensely. He nearly danced over to the hotplate.

"I'm going to have some coffee. You? No? Well now, Thax—why would I want to put anything in your drink?"

"Because I bunked with Terry Orme, and because you wanted me blotto when you paid our tree house a visit that night."

Mike's eyes watched me brightly over the rim of his coffee cup.

"You can tell a story better than that, surely. You mustn't start in the middle, you know. That's using the narrative-hook form and that's cheating."

I was agreeable. "All right, I'll back up to the beginning. You fell for May. Or maybe I should extend that and say you fell for May *and* her husband's money. But the husband was in the way. To eliminate him was no great problem. The rub was that as soon as he turned up murdered everybody would immediately point the finger at May—because of the money motive. So in your somewhat warped ingenious way you worked out a neat little scheme."

Mike sipped his coffee and smiled at me. He said nothing.

"You would murder Cochrane and you would frame it to fit May. But the frame would be so goddarn obvious that even a blindman would be able to recognize it when it started to smell. Why would she use her own knife? And why would she leave her knife in the body? And why would she be so damn careless as to drop her earring by the body? And why wouldn't she at least have enough sense to get herself an alibi for the time of the murder?"

I shook my head.

"It would be too much for anybody to swallow. The law would play with it for a while and then they would set her aside and start looking around for another suspect with a motive. May would be a nice innocent rich widow—all for you."

I looked at him.

"You like it?" He flashed a grin at me. "I always did. But go on. You're telling it."

"Well, you realize I'm just fumbling over the finer details now. This is mostly guesswork, so stop me if I'm wrong."

"You're doing fine, just fine, Thax."

"I don't think you had set an actual date for Cochrane's murder. You were probably still trying to iron out the various wrinkles in your bent little brain—until the day I showed up. You knew my past history and I must have looked like a natural to you. The jealous ex-husband, deadbroke and with a vengeful heart. Good. You decided to hit Cochrane that same night."

I took out a cigarette and rolled it between my fingers.

"Guessing again now, I think you made a date with old man Cochrane for after closing time. Probably told him you had a brand new scheme for Treasure Island and you wanted him to meet you and kick it around. He agreed. He'd come out to the *Hispaniola* late that night. But you didn't want to do him in that close to your homebase. So when he came down to the Admiral Benbow dock, you were already waiting for him in the tearoom."

Mike watched me, beaming expectantly.

"The lights would be out, of course," I said, thinking about it.

"You would call him over to the tearoom on some pretense or other. He steps through the door into pitch darkness and you're there waiting with the knife. Bingo."

"Do you need a light for that cigarette, Thax?"

"It's all right. I've got one."

"Don't let me interrupt you, then. It's fascinating."

"Isn't it? And it gets better." I fished out a match and lit up.

"So. Then you tote him into one of the rowboats and you row across the lake in the dark and you cart him over the little stretch of land and dump him in the Swamp Ride. With May's knife still in him, of course. And you remember to plant May's jade earring in the mudbank where any stumble-bum cop will find it. Then back to the *Hispaniola* and the black coffee and insomnia."

I grinned at him. "You know, I couldn't quite pin you at first."

"How's that, Thax?"

"I mean all the highstrung energy. It's obvious that you're on something, but I never put you down as needle nuts. It's Bennys, huh? Or Dexamyl or Dexedrine? That's the reason for all the black coffee. It keeps activating the pep pills. How do you keep going without sleep though?"

He placed a hand over his heart and spoke dramatically. "A man in love needs no sleep." Then he laughed at himself. "As long as you've interrupted your narration, let me ask you this. Why didn't I just leave the body in the tea room?"

"Um. That's one of the things that started me thinking about you as a possible suspect. Look what happened in *Treasure Island.* Everyone figured the treasure should be in Flint's cache because all the facts pointed to that conclusion. But when they got there they drew a blank, because foxy old Ben Gunn had already picked up the loot and moved it somewhere else. Dandy joke."

I said, "That's *your* style, Mike. You love a good laugh at other people's expense. That business of leaping out at me like Ben Gunn, and of boasting about jumping out on all the little girls and making them wet their panties. You like to shock people, Mike. You like to hit 'em with a startling surprise and then stand back and laugh. And you love a risk. You're the kind of nut who actually enjoys living on the edge of disaster. Like that gamble you took with Bill Duff in the poker game. That was pure brinksmanship.

Mike laughed delightedly.

"Will you ever forget the look on Bill's face? Good old Bill! But go on, Thax. I'm enjoying this."

I knew he was. Because the whole thing, the way he had laid it out—was another big risk. And I had an idea that he had an ace in the hole. I even thought I knew the color of the ace.

"There was no reason on earth to move that body," I said. "You did it for pure shock value. If you'd left it in the tea-room the first waitress who opened up in the morning would walk in and see it and go *Gaa!* Not much fun in that. Just one person. But if you dumped it in the Swamp Ride you could really raise the roof.

"Just picture it," I said. "A whole boatload of happy marks *oh*ing and *ah*ing along the waterway. Then they turn the bend and what do they see floating in the water?"

Mike laughed and slapped his hands.

"Beautiful!" he said. "And I'm still sick it didn't work."

"Yes," I said dryly, "what a shame that freckle-faced kid squelched all the fun." I pitched my cigarette butt through the stern window and said, "So now we come to Terry Orme.

"Just when you figured you'd pulled a perfect crime, blackmail walked in and put the screws on you. So you knew there had been a witness but you didn't know *who.* Then I accidentally gave you a tip when I told you Orme bunked in the tree house. Sure, you figured. Orme is always climbing around in the dark, peeking in on other peoples' business. Orme *had* to be the witness. So . . ."

"So you helped me out by walking in here and asking for a drink."

"Uh-huh. And you doped it and I passed out and then you laid for Orme in the treehouse."

"And then?" Mike prompted me.

"There isn't much more," I said. "Right after Terry took the big drop is when I put on my thinking cap and my thoughts slowly turned me in your direction. So I had to be eliminated next."

Mike was smiling at me. He said nothing.

"But that was the big slip up," I said. "Because *you* didn't handle it. If you had, I'd probably be one day dead right now."

"Go ahead," Mike said. "Tell us why I didn't handle it."

"Because I figure you didn't even know about it, Mike. And the person who did was already too panicky to have a third murder turn up on the lot. So she hired some big city badboys to do the deed in some far-out remote spot.

I looked at the louvered wardrobe across the cabin.

"Is that right, May?" I said.

There was a pause and then both louvered doors swung noiselessly open and May stood there as gorgeous as a George Petty picture, in a bright, tight red outfit that accentuated her flame hair. She was holding one of her pearl-handled knives.

Chapter Eighteen

"You're so goddam smart, darling," May said to me in her stainless steel voice. "It's simply breathtaking to listen to you."

"Maybe I can get a job with Ferris," I said.

"I don't see how, darling," May said. "I really don't. Because I don't think you're going to be for hire much longer. Hasn't your brilliant mind figured out *why* we lured you out here tonight?"

"Um. I think I can make a guess as to how both of you *thought* I'd react once I saw Mike's summmons. You figured I'd rush out here and tell you all I know—which I have just done—and then I'd make a play at holding you up for blackmail. Which isn't a part of my plan."

Mike raised his brows at me. "Is this a rib, Thax? You honestly never intended to make a stab at blackmail?"

"I honestly never did, Mike. Oh sure, I'd like a big chunk of May's dough for keeping my mouth shut, but it won't work. The deal has already gone sour. There's too many angles to it. Too many people have tried to climb on the bandwagon. Sooner or later it's bound to come apart at the seams. I don't want to be inside the bag when it does."

I watched May's hand—the one with the knife.

"Let's face it," I said. "You baited the trap with blackmail when you drew me out here tonight. But we all know you have something more practical in mind. Like a man I knew said: murder and blackmail are two divergent businesses."

"Then why did you come out here, Thax?" Mike asked.

"Because he's a damn fool!" May said sharply. "He's always been a damn fool. He thinks he can talk his way out of anything."

"That's just about the truth," I admitted. "You see, Mike, I never actually finished anything I ever started to do in my life. But this time I made up my mind I'd see this deal out to the end. And speaking of the end . . ."

I leaned forward as if to stand up. In the next instant I had May covered with the automatic.

"Better drop the knife, May," I said.

Mike lowered his coffee cup to the table. He said, "You wouldn't really kill us, would you, Thax?"

I watched May. "Well, turnabout is fair play, isn't it? May—didn't you hear what I said?"

"Certainly, sweetie," May said. She started to raise the knife.

You don't try to talk a rattler out of striking. I pulled the trigger at her.

The hammer said *click.* I was all tensed for the expectant blast and the stupid thing said *click!*

Mike grinned at me.

"Wet powder, Master 'Awkins?" he asked in an Israel Hands voice.

I looked at May. She was smiling and her lips were very moist and scarlet and her eyes very bright. She cocked the knife over her shoulder.

"Catch, May!" I flipped the automatic to her underhand.

The knife went *thh-ok* in the sternpost by my head as I went out the window—going right on over in a backwards somersault through the moon-swerving night and crashing feet-first into the black shallows.

The muck underfoot was mushy and it sloped and the impetus of my plunge threw me into a wet pratfall. I came up thrashing and spitting out a mouthful of that damn duck-doodoo water and stood up with the lake to my waist and looked up at the *Hispaniola's* counter.

Mike Ransome was standing at the center window and wrenching the knife free of the sternpost. His teeth flashed down at me and then he darted back into the cabin.

He was going to cut me off from the rowboat. I wasn't

much as a swimmer and that was out anyhow because if I tried it he could quickly overhaul me in the boat. So I slogged ashore and headed for the underbrush.

A scud of clouds passed over the moon's face—in a hurry, as if it had been waiting for just this to happen. It suited me. If I couldn't see Mike, he couldn't see me. I crawled a little way up Mizzenmast Hill, sticking close to the brush, and stalled to sound the darkness below for danger.

I couldn't hear him, or anything. The island, the lake, all of Neverland and the whole damn world beyond seemed to be one immense silence. That suited me too, but Mizzenmast Hill did not. It was too open. I needed the black shelter of tall trees.

I crawled again, working around the base of the manmade hill and heading inland. I figured I would slip out of my clothes and chance swimming for it, once I reached the far side of the island.

The ground flattened out and the trees loomed and I stopped making like an animal and stood up. The ground was velvety and springy under my feet, carpeted with dead pine needles and leaves and mold. I started walking.

Clawing branches and soft lacy things kept brushing at my face and body and it was so godawful dark in there I couldn't avoid them. I started groping along with my right hand stretched out and it was a damn good thing because right off the bat my palm collided with a tree trunk that had been intended for my nose.

All at once I was trapped. Turn right or left or try to go forward and I was fumbling against trees and branches or blundering into a catclaw thicket. I felt like a blind-man who couldn't find the right path in a hedge maze. I thought about striking a match but vetoed it because a light in that black thicket would stand out.

I put both hands in front of me and had another blind try at finding an opening by Braille.

My outstretched left hand came against something that was soft and giving. It was covered by cloth. I felt one of the buttons.

There was a sharp intake of breath right next to me and I heard or sensed a sudden slash of motion in the dark as I sprang back and crouched for another spring, anywhere, tense and expectant.

Nothing happened. A minute dragged by like a hurt turtle and still nothing happened and I knew Mike was crouching and waiting without sound or movement only a few feet away.

The stillness came apart with a sudden good-god whir of wings as a preying owl made his shrill-laugh cry. I jumped on my nerves and shifted to the right and heard Mike leap forward with a whisk of leaves and then I whirled in another direction and crouched again.

We waited. Nothing happened. I listened for his breathing but he must have been doing it through his mouth. I hunkered down and felt the ground with my right hand. It would be too damn much to ask to find a stick or a rock for a weapon so I carefully scooped up a handful of dirt.

I straightened up. There was no sound.

Without warning a bright flare of light snapped open like a bomb burst and I saw Mike standing six feet away. He had a match in his left hand and May's knife in his right and the blade shone with the thin red light from the match dancing along the edge like blood.

Mike was grinning at me and his thin, moist face looked satanic in the yellowy light. That crazy bastard was having the time of his life.

"Jim,"—he was playing Israel Hands again—"I reckon we're fouled, you and me, and we'll have to sign articles."

He made a quick snatching motion with his left hand to whip out the match and I chucked my handful of dirt at his face as he pounced toward me, and just like that we were in total darkness again and I dropped to the ground in a lump and felt his shins collide on my shoulder, and then I was up and going while Mike was still in a heavy crashing fall in the underbrush.

I broke through an opening between huge-trunked trees by sheer blind luck and started to run and I could hear Mike scrambling right behind me, and just then a christly tree jumped up and I ran smack into it with both arms outflung and all I could do was hug it dazedly like a witless man making love to a knothole.

I felt Mike brush past me in a rush and there was a thud and a rattle of dry branches and a gasp and a sense of something running into nothing and falling through it, and finally a clatter of stones and a throaty cry like *Uuuah!* And then nothing.

I stepped back from the tree I had been loving and felt my face over for something broken. Nothing seemed to be. I took a step forward and stopped. A black patch of mystery fell away in the darkness below me. I was standing on the lip of a ridge. The black patch down at the base was some kind of pit.

I climbed down the slope and realized I was standing in Flint's Treasure Pit. Mike Ransome was there too, but he wasn't standing.

I rolled him over and fished out a match and struck it. The light sparked in his eyes. He was staring up at me but he was seeing something else, somewhere else.

He had put his hands in front of his chest to break his fall. But he had forgotten that May's knife was in his right hand.

Chapter Nineteen

May was pacing up and down through a grayish garland of cigarette smoke when I opened the cabin door. She came to a full, abrupt stop and looked at me and it was a look I had never seen on her face before. Pure shock.

"Thax." She barely said it.

"Why don't you sit down, May?" I said.

I don't think she consciously heard me. She didn't sit down. She didn't make a move. She stared at me and her obsidian eyes seemed to grow in her porcelain-perfect face.

I said, "He's dead, May. He fell on your knife."

She kept staring at me and her black pupils glowed with a dull red light.

"You filthy bastard," she whispered.

"I wouldn't lie to you now, May. If I'd killed him I'd admit it. But I didn't. It was an accident."

Then she sat down, all at once, and it was a good thing the table bench was right behind her or I think she would have gone out on the deck. She seemed to have forgotten the cigarette that was smoking itself between her pale, tapered fingers. She looked blankly at the floor.

"I loved him."

I think she was telling herself, and I think she meant it. At least I think she thought she meant it, which made it just about the same thing. I went over and picked up Gabby's automatic and shoved it under my belt.

"What are you going to do?" She didn't look at me.

"Tell Ferris. I want out of this thing with a clean slate."

She looked at me. "He won't believe you."

"I think he will. He isn't stupid, you know, May. I think he just needed a little more time to get it sorted out. A good cop doesn't like to jump until he has all the facts down pat."

Her cigarette must have started to burn her fingers. She looked at it as if wondering what it was doing there. Then she dropped it on the floor and tapped at it with one red pump.

"Should I run, Thax?" It was not May's voice at all. It was quiet, grave, almost detached. I shook my head.

"It's too late to run, May. You couldn't get far enough fast enough. Besides, it doesn't really matter now, does it?"

"No," she said in the same nothing voice, "I guess it doesn't."

I left her sitting in the cabin. I closed the door very quietly and then I gathered up the rowboat they had used to reach the island and the one I had used and I tied the bow of the one to the stern of the other and rowed back to the Admiral Benbow dock.

The moon was just starting to come out from behind the black scud for another look around. It was nearly three A.M.

They burnt the trash every night in a big furnace room behind the bunkhouse and I made a trip over there because it seemed like a good place to dry out my soggy clothes.

Nobody was in the baked room but an old man asleep on a blanket pallet. He had been making love to a gin bottle and he had neglected to put the cap back on it and there was that ginny perfume scent in the hot air that I could do without.

I capped his bottle for him. If it had been anything except gin I would have had a snort. I have no scruples when it comes to booze.

It didn't take long for my duds to dry out in that heat, and when I was dressed again I went over to the bunkhouse to use the phone.

Four or five of the rummies were sleeping it off in there but they were too far gone to be bothered by the electric light I snapped on.

A typical POed desk-sergeant voice told me no, Ferris wasn't at headquarters and what did I expect at that time of night, or maybe I didn't know what time of night it was?

I told him yes, I knew and that I also knew that another man had just been killed at Neverland and I thought maybe Ferris might want to be cut in on it.

The desk sergeant's voice got excited and he wanted to know who I was and who was killed and who had done it and everything except the color of my socks, and I kept asking for Ferris until finally he gave in grudgingly and switched the call to Ferris' home.

Mrs. Ferris answered and she was sleepy and mad and she said yes, her husband was there but didn't I know what time of night it was? Then Ferris came on by growling yeah?

I told him about it, most of it. How I had figured the plot and how I had gone over to Treasure Island and presented it to May and Mike and how they had tried to kill me.

Ferris didn't get very excited about the news. He said huh. Then he said, "You were just about one giant step ahead of me."

"You mean you had already figured them for it? Mike Ransome in with May Cochrane?"

"Well, I was just rounding that bend," Ferris said. "We got a healthy line on them last night. Seems for the past two-three months they've been renting a room here in town under the name of Mr. and Mr. Millard Rankin. From all indications they'd shack up there whenever old man Cochrane's back was turned. That sort of put the whole deal in a new light."

There was a pause on his end, and then he said, "I take it things went sour for you tonight, huh?"

"How's that?"

"Well, I'll tell you, Thaxton. I get the impression you

went out there with some idea of blackmail in mind. What happened? You couldn't come to terms? That why you're calling cop on them now?"

I let out my breath and shook my head.

"Look," I said, "you're forgetting that I'm supposed to be a rapist, not an extortionist. But believe it or not, none of us had blackmail in mind. They were on to me and they set up a trap to eliminate my troublesome personality. I went out there with the idea I could outfox them, but it misfired on me."

"Yeah," Ferris said and I could tell from his tone just how much he believed me. "So then Ransome accidentally falls on his own knife. Uh-huh. And how did your ex-wife accidentally kill herself?"

"She didn't. She's still out there."

"How's that?"

"I left her on the island."

"Jesus! You just walked off and left her there?"

"It's all right," I said. "I took both rowboats and she doesn't know how to swim. She'll keep."

He said it again, "Jesus. Did it ever enter your goddam head that she might commit suicide?"

"Yes," I said. "Yes, it entered my head. I don't think she will but it's a possibility. But it doesn't really matter, does it? It would save everyone a lot of grief, wouldn't it?"

It was his turn to blow his breath. I heard him do it.

"Thaxton—I'll be out there just as quick as I can find my pants and a squad car. You stay right where you are. Hear me? You and I are going to have a long, hard father and son talk today."

"I've still got a couple of things to take care of," I told him.

His voice leaped along the wire.

"Goddammit, Thaxton, I said *stay where you are!*"

"Take it easy, Ferris. You know where to find me when you want me." I hung up.

One of the rummies woke up and yelled at me to turn off the goddam light. I told him to go —— himself. He didn't but he rolled over and went back to sleep. I looked up Billie's number in the directory.

There was no answer. I figured she was dead asleep and I

let it ring a dozen times but there was still no answer. I repeated the old Anglo-Saxon word I'd just said to the rummy and hung up and walked out of the bunkhouse.

It was getting on to four by the time I reached the basement in Dracula's Castle. I asked the lookout on the door if Gabby was still in the game and when he said yes, I said tell him I wanted to see him out in the hall a minute.

Gabby was wearing insomnialike smudges under his eyes when he stepped outside and closed the door after him. He looked at me with a tired, incurious expression and I handed him his automatic.

"Thanks for the loan," I said. "But you better replace the firing-pin. It works better when all the parts are intact."

Gabby looked at the gun in his hand and wet his lips. He didn't say anything, didn't look at me.

He wasn't my big by a damn sight, but I didn't mind taking him apart because I knew he was a handy little bastard and even if he didn't have a switchblade on him at least he had that Roscoe to use as a sap and that would help equalize our size.

But he just stood there, staring at that gun that wasn't a gun, waiting for it like a convicted war criminal waiting for the inevitable noose. Then he said something that was so incongruous to his nature it caught me offbase.

"Forgive me, Thax."

And then I knew I couldn't do it and that made me feel so goddam mad and frustrated I started yelling at him.

"*Why the hell did you do it?* We were friends, weren't we?"

He let out his breath like a weary man lowering a heavy burden.

"Are they dead?" he asked. "Did you kill 'em?"

"Who? Mike and May? Mike is, and the johns are coming for May."

"Well," Gabby said, and for a long moment I didn't think he was going to say anything else. Then he started to talk.

"They had me in a bind, Thax, and I didn't have enough guts to get up off the ground and make like a man. About four years back me and May worked for the same outfit up north. There was a beef one night on the lot and a mark got killed. I sapped too hard. A few of the carnys knew who did it but they figured the rube had it coming so they clammed up. May was one of 'em."

He grunted with disgust.

"I should have known better. Should have known May better. I came here a couple of years back and got a job with Cochrane. I didn't know that May was his wife or that she was even on the lot. Then one day she walks by my gallery and looks at me. That's all, just looks. No sign, no word. But I knew then she was going to make me pay somehow, sometime. Every day for two years I've waited for the ax to fall. And it finally did—a couple a three days back.

"Mike Ransome came to see me. He gave me this toy. He knew that you and me had become buddy-buddy and he had an idea that before very long you'd be looking around for a gun. He figured you'd come to me and said I was to give you this Roscoe. Said it was all a part of a joke he was going to pull on you and that I'd better help with my end of it unless I wanted the law to take another healthy look at that four year old murder. So . . ."

He raised his head and for the first time since I had known him a look of urgent appeal came into his sallow face.

"But at least I tried to head you off, didn't I, Thax? I told you not to take the damn thing—to cut and run instead."

"That's right, Gabby" I said. "You tried."

I felt empty, disillusioned. I had thought of Gabby as one of those self-contained characters who would always stand up and spit in the world's mean face. Now I saw he had never been anything but a frightened little man.

"Let's forget it," I said. "It doesn't matter now."

But I knew that neither of us could forget it and that nothing would ever be the same again. Gabby knew it too. He didn't say a word when I turned and went up the steps.

I knew I'd be in for a long hard day once Ferris got his hooks in me and started scrubbing me over the washboard, and I didn't want to go into all that without a little sleep under my belt. It was after four by then and I was out on my feet. But I couldn't go back to the tree house because Ferris would send his storm troopers there first thing.

Then I remembered the unused room up in Dracula's Castle. I went up there and closed the door and threw myself on the bed. The last thing I heard was the wailing police sirens coming from a long long way off.

Chapter Twenty

Well, *and where are they now?* Silver was saying. *Pew was that sort and he died a beggarman. Flint was and he died of rum at Savannah. Ah, there was a sweet crew, they was, only where are they Thax. Thax wake up Thax. . .*

Someone was pulling me out of my dream by my shoulder. I opened my eyes and day was smiling through the archer's cross and Billie was standing over me not smiling.

Her eyes were very wide and dark and her face looked pallid. She was wearing a little V of worry between her plucked brows.

"Thax, I've been looking everywhere for you! And so have the police. How long have you been up here?"

I sat up and reached for a cigarette but changed my mind when I remembered that they had had a bath in that ducky lake.

"What time is it?"

"It's nearly nine. Thax, there's policemen all over the place."

I said, "Where were you last night, or early this morning? I tried to phone you."

"I was right here. I never went home. When you didn't meet me at the gate I went over to the tree house to see what had happened to you. I saw your shirts and things on the floor so I stayed there to wait for you. Then I guess I fell asleep. Some policeman woke me up over an hour ago. He was looking for you."

"Do you have a cigarette?"

She sat down on the edge of the bed and gave me one from her purse. She said, "Thax—they're saying that Mike Ransome was killed last night."

"That's right. He had an accident and fell on one of May's knives."

"May Cochrane? What happened to her?"

I looked at her. "Nothing that I know of. The last I saw of her she was sitting in the *Hispaniola* in a daze waiting for the law to come cart her away."

Billie made a little impatient shake with her head.

"I don't understand, honey. What—"

"Mike and May killed old man Cochrane," I said. "Mike did the dirty work. But right off the bat they discovered there had been a witness—when blackmail reared its ugly head. And that's when things started to get messy."

"Blackmail?" Billie said. "You mean there's been a blackmailer in on this murder all along? Who? Bill Duff?"

I really wanted a toothbrush more than a cigarette. It tasted like a freshly printed newspaper. I got up and pitched it out the window.

"Duff," I said, "had an idea what it was all about, and he certainly had blackmail on the brain. But he couldn't get off the ground with it because he lacked a vital part. He didn't have a witness."

"A witness? You mean the blackmailer had a witness to Rob Cochrane's murder?"

I turned and looked at her.

"That's right, Billie. You did have one for a while, didn't you?"

She sat rigidly composed with her legs together and her hands folded in her lap. Her eyes were still very wide, very dark.

"That really isn't very funny, Thax," she said.

"No," I agreed, "it isn't. I stopped laughing some time back."

I reached in my pocket and drew out the envelope I had taken from Lloyd Franks' safe. The dip in the lake had given it a puffy look and the ink had smeared some but it was still legible. I handed it to Billie.

She looked at the envelope, at the words written across the face, of it: *To be opened only in the event of my death—Billie Peeler.* It had been sealed originally but I had opened it after I lifted it and so Billie knew that I knew that the page of paper inside was blank. She put the envelope in her purse and looked at me.

"Terry Orme," I said, "was a bitter, lonely little guy who hated people, normal people. I think in his bent little way he thought he was getting even with them by spying on their personal lives—gave him a superior feeling. I'm just guessing about this, but I figure he knew about May and Mike shacking up, and the night he saw Mike dump

Cochrane in the Swamp Ride he was clever enough to put two and two together.

"It meant money to him, you see? Big money. And May could afford it. But the rub was he was afraid to approach them personally. Can you picture a gutless midget walking up to a tall murderer and saying, I'm going to blackmail you, buster? So he needed a go between. Someone who had the courage and intelligence to tackle blackmail and get away with it."

I put my hands in my pockets and started to make like Ferris, pacing from window to door and back again. Billie followed me with her eyes.

"You were one of the very few people the sad little bastard liked," I told her. "You used to work together in Kansas City and he probably knew you were a shrewd cooky who would stop at nothing to grab a bundle. So he told you about Mike and May—dumped the whole package in your lap and probably asked for fifty-fifty. Or did you get him down?"

Billie said nothing. She watched me.

"Probably the only stipulation Terry made was that you wouldn't tell Mike or May that he was the witness. Which is the way you would have played it anyhow because you *are* a shrewd cooky.

"That first night I asked you for a date you said you had to do some paperwork. You were going to write down just what Terry had seen and told you and seal it in a not-to-be-opened-unless envelope and turn it over to some lawyer. That would be your safeguard against Mike and May. They'd be afraid to touch you with that hanging over their heads.

"But nearly every blackmailer thinks of that angle, and they always warn their marks that they've done it even when probably half of them haven't. And you knew that Mike was the kind of nut who just might gamble that you hadn't put anything on paper, and go ahead and risk eliminating you. So you put a curve on your pitch. You made out the envelope and sealed a blank piece of paper in it and turned it over to Lloyd Franks. . . remember I met you coming from his office the next day?"

Billie watched me.

"Then you told May what you had done and said she and Mike could check with Franks if they didn't believe you. The reason you didn't put anything on paper is because you weren't certain just how far you could trust Franks.

"That's the one trouble with mixing murder and blackmail—lack of trust. Terry wasn't absolutely certain he could trust you. That's why he got so jumpy. He was scared pea-green that you might cross him and tell Mike that he was your witness, and then Mike would kill him. Well—as we both know, Mike *did* find out and he did take care of the little guy. Um—that reminds me. You made a slip that day. You referred to Terry's death as murder, when everyone else assumed it was an accident. But you knew better. Also, it put you in a bit of a bind.

"Mike was a good chessplayer. The most damaging hold you had over him was that eyewitness. Once he had removed that player from the board all you had against him was hearsay evidence. However, you were still a threat to them because you could tell the law all you knew even if you couldn't prove any of it. So I figure they agreed to go ahead and pay you off in one lump sum for your nuisance value."

I stopped my stroll and looked at her.

"I take it May told you you'd have to wait a couple of weeks until she could find a valid excuse to dig into her husband's estate for the ante. How much was it by the way?"

"One hundred thousand," Billie said promptly and calmly.

"You ever see any of it?"

"One fourth. May had that much cash of her own." Billie dug in her purse for a cigarette. "Let me have a light, Thax."

"Mine won't work. I shampooed them in the lake last night. Let me get this straight. You have twentyfive thou in cash?"

"That's right, darling," Billie said. She found her own match. Then she blew smoke toward me.

"We can leave any time," she said.

"Leave? Where?"

"Here. For the Mediterranean. Just as we planned."

I stared at her. I said, "You're kidding."

She said, "I don't see why I should be. We're clean. No one has anything on us. We didn't murder anyone."

I let out my breath.

"Billie. My dear ex-wife didn't know I was on to her and her Peter Pan boyfriend until someone told her I was getting warm. And you, dear heart, were the only person who knew it."

Billie stared at me through the smoke swirl. Then she dropped her cigarette on the floor and stood up.

"Thax, I wanted that money so damn badly. Don't you understand, honey. You get a chance like this once in a lifetime. I loved you—but I couldn't let anything happen to that money. That's why I went to May, to warn her, to—"

"To have her come unstitched and hire some hoods to eliminate me," I said.

"No!" she cried. "I never dreamed she'd do anything like that. I thought she'd try to buy you off. I thought you'd be reasonable and. . ." Her voice trailed off and she averted her eyes and put her lower lip between her teeth. Her eyes started to go moist.

"Jesus," I said quietly, looking at her. "I must have seemed like a real Prince Charming to you. Did you really think I'd take it from May, even if she'd been silly enough to offer it?"

"Thax," she murmured. "Thax."

I walked back to the archer's cross and looked down at Neverland. Three or four of Ferris' storm troopers were hurrying about in the near distance, but other than that everything looked bright and peaceful, like a great enchanted land where once long ago men had toiled and built and dreamed and then gone away.

"Billie—I think you'd better start to run now."

"What?"

I turned and looked at her and I felt dead.

"It always comes out in the wash, Billie. So you don't have much time. You'd better take your twentyfive grand and run with it just as fast and as far as you can go. And if you're lucky—maybe you'll even reach the Mediterranean."

Her eyes reminded me of May's eyes. That same dull red gleam back in the pupils.

"You won't come with me?"

"No. Because I could never trust you."

"You stupid fool!" she cried. "You'll never be anything but a carny bum if you stay here. We both have a chance if you'd come with me. We could—"

"You'd better start, Billie. It's later than you think."

She stood glaring at me with those very wide eyes of hers, breathing heavily through her mouth. Then something which must have had to do with her sense of the inexorable relaxed inside her and she closed her mouth and her eyes and gave a small, hopeless shake with her head and turned away.

She stopped and fumbled in her purse, brought out a pack of cigarettes and her book of matches and tossed them on the bed.

"You'll need those," she said tonelessly. "You always seem to be out of matches or something."

"Thanks," I said. It took the place of goodby.

I listened to her heels click down the steps until they were only an echo in my mind. Then I roused myself and went downstairs into the clean bright strength of the new day.

The first influx of marks was starting to pour into the lot when I reached my stand. Gabby was behind his counter and we looked at each other and then he looked away. Bill Duff was on his bally, waiting, and he exchanged a blank glance with me and that was that.

Down at the far end I saw the young new breed dick marching toward me like a soldier on a sacred mission. I made a slow pass with the walnut shells, right over left and switched shells.

"And here they go again, gentlemen!" I called. "Three little medicine bottles with Dr. Thaxton's famous remedy pill that is guaranteed to cure your girl's blues. Step aside, folks. Let the man see the rabbit."

After all, it didn't really matter, did it?

About the Author

Robert Edmond Alter was the author of fourteen children's books and three adult novels, *Swamp Sister*, *Carny Kill* and *The Red Fathom*. His stories appeared in numerous magazines including *Adventure*, *Saturday Evening Post* and *Argosy*. He died in Los Angeles, where he lived, in 1966 at the age of forty.

Printed in Great Britain
by Amazon

43923456R00088